I grabbed my backpack, then ducked my head and ran clear of the rotors. The pilot's eternal grin widened yet again and he gave me a thumbs-up before lifting off, leaving me the lone intruder in the vast quiet of the great land.

I allowed myself to think about my kids just then and to wonder whether I was out of my mind. With their father dead, Jake and Jessie Maxwell might end up orphans. One parent down and one to go. And the one they had left hung out in locales known to be frequented by man-killing beasts and murderers. For what?

The answer to my question suddenly appeared a hundred yards offshore, lit by a triangle of golden light that streamed through a chink in the heavy cloud cover. The pod of whales announced its presence by blowing, spout after spout erupting across the waters of McNeil Cove. A set of flukes lifted from the water—deeply notched in the center and scalloped on the rear margin. Humpbacks. Their paths laced silver seams in the calm water. And then one of the whales breached, heaving its mighty bulk into the air, sea water streaming from its barnacle-encrusted hide before it landed again with a terrific splash.

In my world, there is a place in the sea for whales and a place on the land for grizzlies. For I know with dead certainty that if there is no room on this earth for the wild, then there is no place on the planet for me. . . .

Books by Elizabeth Quinn

Any Day Now
Blood Feud
Murder Most Grizzly

Published by POCKET BOOKS

—A LAUREN MAXWELL MYSTERY—

MURDER MOST GRIZZLY

ELIZABETH QUINN

POCKET BOOKS

New York   London   Toronto   Sydney   Tokyo   Singapore

This book is a work of fiction. Names, characters, places and incidents are either products of the author's imagination or are used fictitiously. Any resemblance to actual events or locales or persons, living or dead, is entirely coincidental.

An *Original* Publication of POCKET BOOKS

POCKET BOOKS, a division of Simon & Schuster Inc.
1230 Avenue of the Americas, New York, NY 10020

ISBN: 0-671-74990-0

First Pocket Books printing December 1993

10 9 8 7 6 5 4 3 2 1

POCKET and colophon are registered trademarks of Simon & Schuster Inc.

Cover art by Jeffrey Adams

Printed in the U.S.A.

For Jeffrey
the bear is the river is the edge

Author's Note

The word *doyon* carries special meaning for the Athabascan people and is used as a surname in this novel with all due respect. The characters in my story who carry that name are meant to represent the best of the old and new ways of an ancient culture.

The freshness, the freedom, the farness—

Robert Service

MURDER
MOST GRIZZLY

1

The kill was not fresh. I didn't need any of the book learning or lab learning that went into my Ph.D. to tell me that. My nose did the job, nostrils alerted by the reek and flaring wide before my brain even processed the foul bit of new data: Ripe stench equals dead thing, not fresh. A winter kill, probably, and just what hibernation-starved grizzlies love for breakfast.

I stumbled to a stop on the rough trail that wound through the tufted hillocks of the Mikfik sedge flats. My obligation as a scientist required closer investigation, even though stopping would probably make me late for my rendezvous with Roland Taft. The strong sun of May's lengthening days had burned off the last wisps of fog, and in the distance I could see the serrated ridges of the Aleutian Range for the first time since the floatplane deposited me on the beach at McNeil Cove. Indigo oceans, lavender mountains, turquoise skies—that's Alaska. A vast immensity of beauty that's home to plenty of beasts as well—the

1

cold, the dark, not to mention the bears. Awesome beauties and merciless beasts. My kind of fairy tale.

I swung the day pack off my back and dug through it, finally coming up with the jar of Vicks VapoRub and the fully loaded .45-caliber Colt automatic that are parts of my trail survival kit, thanks to Max. My husband picked up the trick of stuffing the nose full of Vicks while filling body bags in Vietnam. He decided to pack a cannon in the bush after joining a rescue party in Montana that tracked down a camper who was carried off by a grizzly one fine summer night. Since Max didn't believe in making lots of rules, the ones he followed tended to count. The years of our marriage taught me enough respect for those rules that I started warbling a Beatles tune to make sure any creature within earshot knew I was nearby. John, Paul, George, and Ringo are great on the trail because just about everybody knows the words and nostalgia in harmony makes it easier to forget sore feet.

After smearing a glop of Vicks into my nose, I started along the trail again, checking for fresh scat with each careful step. Not that I really expected to run into a grizzly. All the years I'd lived in the north, the only brown bears I'd ever sighted on the ground wandered into view when I was safely in the air. Which suited me just fine after hearing Max's account of that awful night in 1967. One sleeping camper plus one rogue bear equals massive trauma. If a single swipe from a grizzly forepaw can fracture the skull of a bull elk, imagine what *Ursus arctos horribilis* did to a pretty college girl from Minnesota. I didn't expect to meet one, but, just in case, I had the .45 ready as I picked my way forward.

Outside of the safety tips I'd learned from Max, the

little I knew about grizzlies came from Roland Taft. Like the fact that bears prefer following an established trail for the same reason humans do: It's easier walking. Or that the grizzly joins man, rats, and hogs in being a true omnivore willing to eat just about anything. Of course, just as my culinary downfall is fats—McDonald's french fries, pepperoni pizza, king crab dipped in butter—the grizzly also exhibits dietary preferences, particularly for berries and fish. Which explains why the McNeil River's legendary salmon runs attract grizzlies each summer and also bear scientists like my friend Roland.

I nudged a pile of scat with the toe of my boot. Firm meant not fresh. Like the kill. The first white grizzly slayer, a Hudson's Bay Company explorer named Henry Kelsey, was told not to eat the bear by natives who said it was God. Roland's voice had held an almost religious fervor as he tried to convince me to drop everything in Anchorage and fly down to see him. RIGHT NOW! What he didn't tell me was why. The connection wavered into static. Something about the bears. Missing? And then an instant of clarity. "Follow the trail up the Mikfik toward the lake, and I'll meet you near there." Before I could respond, he'd gone, leaving my ear tuned to the hollow hum that runs like an undercurrent through every radio patch.

Around the next hillock I came upon the killing ground. Massive blood loss stained the fresh green sedges a rusty brown, matting the plants against earth still damp with spring runoff. Four-inch claws had disemboweled the prey with one swipe, spilling organs and intestines for the smaller creatures, which still fluttered and buzzed above the feast. Sharp canines had punctured the limbs, tearing skin from flesh, ripping flesh from bone, scattering a piece here and another one there. Complete mutilation, except for the head. Even the vagaries of sun and weather and ravenous beasts could not disguise the texture of the hair or the shape of the eyes.

I turned away as weakness swept over me, buckling my knees while the gorge rose in my throat and emptied onto the spring green of the Mikfik sedge flats. One of Alaska's great beauties, complete with the bloody handiwork of one of her lurking beasts— all that was left of my friend Roland Taft.

2

Roland Taft was a late bloomer, as a scientist and as a man. I met him when we were both lab rats at SUNY Buffalo, a good enough school as state universities go but certainly no scientific dynamo like MIT or Stanford. Back then, Roland was what my kids would call a geek. I guess I was, too. In the late sixties, science was definitely OUT. What was IN was culture and social consciousness, meaning "disciplines" like literature or history or political science where savvy students could spew out fifteen pages of hip bullshit and pull an A in the course. Since biology wasn't cool on campus in those days, none of the other girls bothered to look too closely at Roland so none of them noticed his similarity to the Marlboro man— silky blond thatch, lapis-blue eyes, firmly sculpted chest. I sure noticed. Eventually I made a pass but retreated with wounded dignity in the face of his shock and alarm. I'd figured any biology major knew the facts of life, but to this day I'm still not certain that Roland really grasped what I was after.

Like I said—a late bloomer. Scientifically, too. For the longest time he couldn't find a focus for his research. One semester he'd be noodling around with rats, and the next he'd be glued to the eyepiece of the department's electron microscope. By temperament, Roland was a generalist, the kind of guy who'd make a great utility science teacher for a small-town high school, dissecting worms in a morning biology class and brewing on a Bunsen in the afternoon chemistry class. The summer I headed west to Berkeley, Roland landed a job as a gofer for some bear researchers heading to Alaska. And was he jazzed! Roland's big adventure—camping out all summer in the middle of God knows where doing all the scut work for a pair of legendary prima donnas. The rest, as they say, is history. Just like Roland.

I slowly worked my way back toward the beach at McNeil Cove, tearing narrow strips off the bottom of my yellow T-shirt to flag the trail. About every dozen yards I tied a scrap around a handful of sedge so that whoever came out to deal with the remains of my friend could find him pretty easily. Maybe marking the trail was my attempt to impose order on the chaos of Roland's death. I guessed that state officials would take the lead in the investigation since the death occurred within the bounds of the state's McNeil River Sanctuary. I knew from my years with Alaska Fish and Game that death by bear mauling automatically triggered an inquiry complete with written policies and standard procedures. The last one I could remember had been a year or so earlier, a girl dragged out of a tent in Katmai National Park, not far from the McNeil River. Another scientist, ironically. Or rather, a scientist-to-be, another of the college students who'd been hired to collect data for one of the zillion ongoing studies of the long-term effects of the *Exxon Valdez* oil spill on wildlife. A birder, I thought, probably studying bald eagles.

Ripping and tying, ripping and tying, I finally came back within sight of the sea, still singing Beatles songs but not enjoying it anymore. Each time I stopped to leave a marker, I also scanned for bears. Like bureaucrats, scientists are methodical and great believers in procedure. Amend that to read "most scientists." Roland wasn't. After losing out in the competition for an official research job at McNeil River, he stayed on anyway, building a squatter's cabin somewhere up one of the drainages and even wintering over. What British imperialists termed going native. In Alaska it's known as subsistence living. Every once in a while a paper of his would show up in one of the appropriate scientific journals and remind the bean counters in Juneau that they hadn't factored a nuisance named Roland Taft into their management plan for the McNeil River ecosystem. Then the memos would start flying all over again, demanding that the researchers who came on-scene every summer track down the rogue and dispose of him. The on-scene guys would then fall back on the sit-on-your-hands procedure until the jerks at the capital forgot about Roland again. The scientists at McNeil viewed Roland's impact on the ecosystem as harmless. Besides, good company is scarce in the bush, and Roland *could* recite from memory the entire canon of Robert Service's poetry. Plus he did good science.

Back at the beach, I turned toward the two battered

cabins where McNeil researchers live in summer. Drifts of snow still checkered the rocks, but draining from each pile was a milky slick of meltwater that trailed glistening into the surf. No rainbow sheen of oil, thank God. This bit of coast had been spared the petroleum devastation visited on much of southwest Alaska when Exxon's tanker crew made their navigational error and ripped their ship open on Bligh Reef. I picked up as much driftwood as I could carry to replenish whatever I'd burn that night. Restocking what you use is not just good manners in the bush, it's also good sense. Think of it as a kind of chain letter where the death threat's for real—a cold stove and no woodpile can add up to tragedy when there's ten feet of soggy snow covering everything. Even though the sun was still high in the afternoon sky, a chill thread already wound through the air. I noticed that clouds had started to build in the northeast, either incoming weather or another eruption of Redoubt volcano. After dumping the first armful of wood in front of the cabins, I went off down the beach to search for more, keeping busy to keep from thinking about what had happened to my friend.

Even when washing grubby urban sands, the ocean soothes me with its inexorable rhythms and relentless tides. Multiply the loveliest beach you've ever seen by a factor of 100, and you get an idea of the incomparable beauty of Alaska's beaches. Too bleak, a greenhorn thinks, until he notices the pod of gray whales swimming just offshore. Too quiet, complains the tenderfoot, just before his step stirs up a cloud of murres that moan hoarsely as they wing along the rocky shore. The water may be too frigid for swimming, but there's never a crowd. At least not of humans.

After gathering enough wood, I shinnied up a pole to the elevated food cache and borrowed two cans of stew, one for supper and one for breakfast. Despite the exertion, the cold finally got to me. Two solid kicks unstuck the door of one cabin and I was home. The stove was standard Alaska issue—the fifty-five-gallon drum that some people think should be named the state flower. Besides being used for cookstoves and heat stoves, those babies come in handy as bathtubs, smokers, doghouses, raft floats, flowerpots, wheelbarrows, culverts, well casings, and just about anything else that you could dream up. I squeezed a four-inch length of fire ribbon out of the tube I carry in my pack, laid on a bunch of dry kindling, and had a roaring fire a lot faster than any Klondike sourdough ever managed. I also carry a flint and can even use it when necessary, but what's the point? No question the first ninety years of this century have produced more horror than all the rest of human history combined, but let's be fair and give some credit. After all, the twentieth century has also produced some worthwhile things. For instance, the smallpox and polio vaccines. And the forty-hour work week. And portable fire starter, of course, plus the Bic lighter to spark it off.

As the shadows of the long spring twilight lengthened, I heated the stew. I even managed two mouthfuls before my mind carried me back to the Mikfik sedge flats. Holding back the horror only works for so long. Idle the mind for a moment and the monster rushes in, looming larger and more fierce than ever. To remain huddled on that stool inside that cabin took every ounce of strength I had. What I wanted more than anything was the bottle I'd spotted in the supply cache. That had been my solution when Max's plane went down—crawl into the booze until you've had enough to kill the memories or the feelings, whichever goes numb first.

I forced myself to breathe slow and deep, counting first to ten and then to a hundred and then to a thousand, until the effort to stay finally chattered my clamped teeth and shook my clasped hands. Tears trailed down my cheeks and fell from my chin, but I couldn't risk freeing my hands long enough to wipe them away. When the initial rush of panic subsided, I forced myself to eat the stew, chewing each tasteless mouthful twenty-five times and then taking a long pull off my water bottle, pausing after each bite to mop up the tears with my sleeve. By the time I'd emptied the saucepan, the worst of it was over. A great weariness flooded through me. Partly from fear of the very real dangers lurking outside in the dark. Partly because since Max died, every loss feels like losing him all over again. I used the last of my energy loading the stove with wood to last through the subarctic night and had just enough reserve to get into my sleeping bag before falling into a deep, dreamless sleep.

Hours later the whine of an engine woke me to the silvery light of dawn. In the few minutes it took me to shake off sleep and wriggle out of my down bag, Cal Williamson had beached his bird and climbed down onto a pontoon to shout. "Hello the cabin. Hello the cabin."

When I opened the cabin door, a smile of recognition creased the grizzle on his cheeks, and he waved a hand toward the roofline. "Spotted the smoke and decided to check. Thought you were bunking with Taft."

A chill dampness leaked through my wool socks as I crossed the rocks. "A bear killed Roland."

Williamson's smile vanished as he jumped down from the pontoon and darted up the beach. He touched my elbow. "You okay?"

"Oh, sure." I tried to keep the tremble out of my voice as his blunt blue stare roved all over me, checking for damage. "I didn't see it happen. Animals had been at him, so it must have been a couple of days ago at least." Fresh tears welled in my eyes. "I marked a trail with yellow flags."

His eyes stopped checking my limbs and searched my face instead, sizing up my potential for hysteria. Old-timers like Cal Williamson prefer to get the job done and get home before coming apart. It's safer that way.

I sniffed hard and dabbed at the tears with the cloth collar on my down vest. "How about getting on your radio while I get my stuff together? Try the state police or Alaska Fish and Game."

He stiffened. A man not used to taking orders sometimes bristles at a mere suggestion, especially one coming from a woman. His eyes sharpened with challenge. "How come you know so much about it?"

Just then a bout of shivers rippled over me, giving me the time I needed to frame a safe response. In my line of work a certain number of full-throated and glaring-eyed encounters of the toe-to-toe variety go with the job. But I hate gratuitous confrontations. They're emotionally draining. And certainly not what I needed after the upheaval of discovering Roland's body.

When my teeth and bones stopped rattling, I gave

Cal Williamson a weak smile, trying to arouse his he-man side. A lot of these old-timers came to Alaska in search of a world where a fellow could lead a manly life and find a grateful gal eager to share it. Instead, what most of them found was a bunch of independent women with agendas of their own who seldom needed the he-man protection and wilderness wisdom of his Little Cabin in the Arctic fantasy. I spread my hands as the smile faded. "I used to work for Fish and Game."

"Used to?" His voice now had an edge that matched the blade in his eyes. "Used to be Fish and Game. Then what are you now?"

This time my smile was genuine. I decided a long time ago that when confrontation is inevitable, you might as well enjoy it. Sometimes being the bogeyman can be fun. Old-time Alaskans greet tree-hugging preservationists with the kind of bug-eyed, hissing outrage fundamentalists reserve for secular humanists of the Satanic variety. "I'm an investigator." For some reason I stuck out my hand. "For the Wild America Society."

Cal Williamson's eyes didn't bug out and he didn't hiss exactly, but the ugliness of his words carried as much venom as any snakebite. "Your kind I hate, loving trees and rocks and dumb animals more than people. Should be you lying out there." A bubble of spit frothed one corner of his mouth as he slapped my hand aside. "Should be you out there dead."

3

***

Some days life overwhelms me. My mother says it runs in the family, especially the women. From one generation to the next our matrilineal descent has included a reputation for energy, intelligence, and common sense. Most of the men could tell you that the down side to such paragons is their tendency to break down. Not as in "nervous breakdown" and never in time of crisis. No, we dynamos choose our down times pretty carefully. My great-grandmother had a couple of bouts of the vapors each year, and her daughter was known for taking to her bed on the vaguest of pretexts.

My mother never even pretended to be ill. I'd come home from school to find her flaked out in her bedroom, the spread littered with magazines and a tray heaped with goodies on the nightstand. On the calendar such days were absolutely empty—no doctor's appointments, dance recitals, church picnics, or PTA meetings. As I helped Dad get a dinner of grilled cheese sandwiches and tomato soup, I'd glance at the blank white square under the calendar's reproduction of a painting by some obscure Impressionist and mentally pencil in "Mom's day off." Around about college I started taking my own days off. Mental health days, I called them, and I never needed one more than the morning after I returned from the McNeil River.

The day before had been wretched. Cal Williamson allowed me to fly out of there with him but made no pretense of his dislike. The glacial silence endured through a stop in Kodiak, where he climbed out of the plane without a word. I needed to use the bathroom in the terminal but didn't dare, fearing he'd grab the opportunity to ditch me. I could complain all I wanted about the three hundred dollars I paid in advance, but no bush pilot worth his wings gives a damn about FAA rules and regulations. After about five minutes he returned, taking great care with the small Gott cooler he carried, placing it gently on the seat beside me and strapping it in. Something fragile, probably medical. Maybe even an organ for transplant. I didn't ask and Cal Williamson didn't say. He also didn't say anything about having notified the authorities of Roland's death.

As soon as we landed in Homer, they swarmed around me—a pack of men claiming to represent the state police, Fish and Game, the division of Wildlife Conservation, the Department of Natural Resources, the Parks and Recreation division—looked like Cal Williamson had rounded up all the usual bureaucrats. Not for the first time, I wished I'd flown down from Anchorage so I'd have a good excuse for escaping.

Having a plane to catch always works in Alaska because absolutely everyone at some time or another has missed one and been forced to wait hours, days, or even weeks for the next flight out. But I have to admit that driving down had been a conscious decision. No matter how long I live in Alaska, I'll never get used to that first view of Kachemak Bay once you get around the last big turn on the Sterling Highway—the glaciered peaks of the Kenai Range tower above a deep-blue sea and, curling into the water like a flower petal unfolding, the Homer Spit.

That's where they fed me—out on the spit at a seafood place with a terrific view of the harbor. At least they let me have a window seat. Even offered to buy me a drink as we went over it and over it. No, I didn't know when it happened. Or how, either, except in the most obvious way—four-inch claws, immense strength. When they asked what I was doing down there, I hedged a little bit. I'm not sure why. Maybe because I wasn't certain why Roland had summoned me. Maybe because I'd somehow sensed something more in his death than simply man versus beast.

Question after question, all basically the same, each phrased just a little differently, a round-robin approach giving each fellow a chance to strut his stuff. They weren't bad guys, really, just trying to do their jobs. McNeil Cove is accessible by boat or plane only at high tide, meaning the scene of Roland's death was unreachable for hours yet, so the official pack did the next best thing and concentrated on their only witness. Me. After almost six hours, just about the time the tide turned, they decided they'd heard enough and thanked me very much, shook my hand firmly, and, to a man, promised to be in touch, leaving me finally free to find my Toyota 4-Runner among the pickups in the parking lot and head on home.

I stuck a Bonnie Raitt cassette into the tape deck and headed north on the Sterling Highway, hoping the music would wash my head free of bad memories. Two hundred and twenty-five miles of pavement leaves a lot of room for thinking. I stopped in Ninilchik to fill my thermos with Russian tea and admire the Orthodox church on a bluff overlooking Cook Inlet, which gleamed silver under a washed-out sky. On through Clam Gulch, Kasilot, Soldotna, and Sterling before stopping again in Cooper Landing, picking up a cheeseburger and fries at Gwin's Lodge to fortify myself for the climb over the mountains to Portage. I called home while my order cooked and, when the machine answered, asked for messages. Nothing. They weren't expecting me until the next morning, so I left a message of my own, saying only that I'd get in around midnight.

I felt better after eating. A tape of the Boston Pops performing a bunch of patriotic ruffles and flourishes took care of the climb up to the pass, and Leonard Bernstein provided some *Sturm und Drang* fireworks for the downhill coast into Portage. I headed the 4-Runner up the Turnagain Arm, sprinting for home, hitting the southernmost streetlights of Anchorage just after eleven and pulling into my darkened driveway in Eagle River just before twelve.

My housemate, Nina Alexeyev, waited for me on the porch, perched on a director's chair and huddled inside a fuzzy blue poncho. "Kids are both asleep. Finally. You know Jake." She uncurled and stood up. "What happened?"

I tried to bluff her, not sure I wanted to get into the horror of Roland tonight. "What do you mean?"

"Come off it, Lauren." She touched my arm gently. "It's in your voice. We were at the clinic when you called, but the answering machine got it. What Jessie heard in your voice started her crying."

One part of me wanted to believe that the mere thought of my baby girl in tears started my own downpour. Another side focused on my housemate's incredible compassion, remembering that Nina's touch could quiet even the most frenzied critter. All bullshit aside, the thing that held back my tears all day was knowing I could safely blubber till doomsday once I got home. Because Nina was there, ready to pick up the pieces. Just the way Max had been. Sort of.

In about five minutes the worst of it passed, leaving me a drippy, hiccuping mess but feeling much better. Nina's little pats and murmurs of encouragement kept rhythm with my sobs, slackening off in matching time. In the last few years she's learned just how quickly my armor goes back on. And how likely I am to wield a cutting tongue if I'm babied too long. I suppose the special tension between us is only natural, to be expected in any friendship where one woman is straight and the other gay.

When Max first mentioned the idea of bringing Dr. Nina Alexeyev into his veterinary practice, I'd been opposed. Even after hearing all of her good points—young, energetic, bright, creative, etc., etc., *ad nauseum*—I kept trying to talk him out of it. One day he finally caught on and called me on it. The tone of his voice should have tipped me off—the same slow, methodical drawl he used when a particularly obtuse client couldn't decide whether to medicate Fifi for heartworm monthly or daily. Another part of his strategy was phoning me at work, where I couldn't use any emotional or sexual wiles to sidetrack the discussion. "Look, kiddo. You can't come up with one good reason why I shouldn't hire Nina Alexeyev," Max said, before launching into another one of his lists. "She's not stupid. She's not lazy. She's not inexperienced. And she's not a drone." A two-beat pause. "She *is* a dyke. And that, although you'll never admit it, is the real objection." Another pause. "Which is your problem. Not hers. And definitely not mine."

Max's great revelation only made things worse. First, because he hired her. And second, because I felt diminished in the eyes of the man I loved. I kept having this vision of Max totting up all of my qualities, sterling and otherwise, and adding a new minus to the debit side of the ledger: irrational fear of dykes. In the years that followed—the last three years of Max's life—I kept my distance from Nina, always cordial but never chummy. She became my husband's friend as well as his partner. And she became a huge influence and loving presence in my children's lives. I had a couple of weird twinges about her relationship to Jessie before finally admitting the fundamental irrationality of my fear. To myself. Never to Max, which is an oversight I'll always regret. And much too late to Nina, who's persevered in the face of my self-destructive grief over losing Max and probably saved my life.

Nina arrived in the first hours that Max's plane was overdue and has never really left. She ran the house while I manned the phone—pestering the air patrol for news, begging anyone with a plane for help in the search, answering endless questions from newspeople representing newspapers, radio, and TV. So many people loved Max. So many people wanted to help. Our friend John Doyon sent up the Tanana Native Corporation's whole fleet of airplanes and his sister, Belle, harnessed up her best dogs and searched the ground. Day after day, nothing. I died in pieces as the hours passed, little bits here and there stiffening up as the love that was the lifeblood of my existence drained away. Not long into the ordeal, I took a drink before facing a press conference. Within days I needed a drink before facing my empty bed. Nina was always there in the background—making sure meals were cooked and kids were hugged and life went on. When I spared a thought for her, I figured she wanted my body. I found out later that what Max's partner really wanted was my family.

After my tears and my liver dried out, I tried to thank her, asking what I could do to repay her kindness. She waved a dismissive hand, blinked a couple of times fast, and said very simply, "I loved Max, too." And then she turned away, hiding her eyes but not the spasm that ran over her shoulders. "I hope I can still spend time with Jake and Jessie. They're the closest I'll ever get to having kids of my own." After hearing that, I took her into my arms and into my family. Survivors are often swept with anger at being left alone. Since that day, my anger at Max for leaving is tempered by gratitude that Nina is among the many things he left behind.

Now I'd faced another ordeal, and again my friend, Nina, was there to help. As I swallowed the last sob, I remembered she'd been at the clinic when I called and wondered why.

"A state trooper brought in a wolf pup." She shook

her head. "Some Pollyanna on a bus tour spotted the little guy up on Mount Alyeska and insisted on bringing him down on the chair lift since he'd lost his mother."

"Meaning somewhere out there a wolf bitch is going nuts, counting and recounting her litter, wondering where she lost him." I dropped my day pack on the couch and sat down beside it to unlace my boots. "Well, her baby'll have to stay with us for a night or two. I'm just too bushed to even think about hiking all over looking for a wolf den. I'm taking tomorrow off as a mental health day."

Nina sighed and shook her head again. "Tough luck, Lauren, but a mental health *morning* is more like it. You're due at the kids' school for a wildlife show at one."

I groaned, but Nina was having none of it. She gave me a brisk pat on the shoulder. "Buck up, sweetie. It's not so bad. At least you don't have to autopsy the bear that ate Roland Taft. I do. They called right after you did."

I shuddered and met Nina's troubled eyes without saying a word. She'd known all along but kept quiet for my sake, letting me get it out in my own way and in my own time. Looked like I'd get to return the favor soon enough.

4

I looked out over the upturned faces of twenty-five wiggling first graders, locked glances with one brown-eyed beauty, and received the emotional boost I needed to compensate for missing out on the second half of my mental health day. My little Jessie gets to me that way. From her shining eyes and gap-toothed smile to her electric blue leggings and scuffed hi-tops, she vibrated with excitement and pride that her mom was today's special treat. Seven years old, high energy, very bright, full of sass—she calls me "Mama" and I melt. What can I tell you? Inside the hard objective shell of the scientist beats the aching heart of a mother whose little girl barely remembers her daddy. You make allowances and find yourself forever changed.

I busied myself with my three pet carriers while Mrs. Welton got her class settled down and ready for the entertainment. I'd chosen today's topic— adaptation—and Nina had taken care of everything else, selecting a fox, an otter, and a mouse to illustrate my lesson and delivering the animals to Jessie's class-room just before one. We may have our disagreements about the efficacy of rescuing individual animals when whole species face extinction through the loss of habitat, but Nina's do-gooding definitely pays off when it comes to community education. Having a warm, furry body to touch turns a largely intellectual argument into something concrete and personal. Once you show them a critter, the discussion moves from animals in general to this mouse or this fox or this otter. Right now otters are very big with the public. Too bad ten thousand of their number had to die in agony in the oily wake of the *Exxon Valdez* before most Alaskans recognized the threat hanging over Prince William Sound.

"All right, children. It's time for our program." I recognized the narrow glance Mrs. Welton shot around the room from my own grade school days and guessed that it takes about thirty years of experience to master the craft of taming the beasts with a single shot of fire from Zeus-like eyes. "A lot of you know Mrs. Maxwell because she's Jessie's mom, but did you know she's a scientist, too? A biologist?"

A head or two nodded, but most of the kids sat goggle-eyed and silent. Except my girl, of course. Jessie glowed. As soon as Mrs. Welton finished her introduction, I zeroed in on the kids.

"I bet you know lots of scientists, don't you?" A freckle-faced redhead buried a fit of giggles behind a slightly grimy fist.

I turned to a skinny boy with a mop of dark curls. "What about you, young man? Do you know many scientists?"

He grinned back at me and shook his head.

"Gee, there must be some mistake." I propped my chin on my hand. "Mrs. Welton and I make two. And then there's all of you. Which adds up to three, four, five . . ." I made a great show of counting heads, touching each child as I moved along the rows. ". . . twenty-five, twenty-six, twenty-seven."

I walked back to the front of the room and folded my arms. "Twenty-seven. I'd call that a lot of scientists."

The giggling redhead waved her arm. "I'm not a scientist."

"You're not?" I stepped forward and frowned. "You mean you never ask questions? You never wonder about stuff? Like why do birds fly? Or how come it snows in the winter? And what makes kitty-cats purr?"

"Well, yes. Sometimes I wonder." The little girl dipped her head and giggled again. "Sometimes I ask questions."

I spread my arms. "Then you're a scientist." Her face lit up. "Asking questions is what scientists do. A scientist's job is to wonder about stuff and then spend a lot of time asking how come."

Television may have dulled more than one generation, but Jessie's crew were still sharp and eager. Given a reasonable level of nourishment and a reasonable amount of attention, most kids are. At seven, anyway. The experience of mothering eleven-year-old Jake had taught me that the put-on blasé of phoney sophistication can hit as young as age nine if the parents are ridiculous enough. I guess I'll never understand why a fan of *Entertainment Tonight* or *Vanity Fair* would choose to live in Alaska. Mysto-squeezo New Agers with crystals and Yuppie back-to-the-landers with satellite downlinks may claim different, but Alaska doesn't choose you. You choose it, and if you survive your first winter, you're *cheechako* no longer. In the great land, tenderfoot is a designation even Cub Scouts despise.

In a very short time we'd progressed from scientists as askers of questions to scientists as framers of hypotheses and were ready for one of our own. I reached into the smallest pet carrier and came up with Hopalong, the Meadow Jumping Mouse. Or, more specifically, Hopalong, the *Zapus hudsonius.* That's how I introduced him when I invited the kids to get out of their seats for a closer look. I knelt on the floor, and they crowded around. One little girl squeaked in fear and another cooed about how cute he was, but most of the kids studied Hopalong for a few seconds before stating the obvious.

"He's pretty little."

"But his tail's pretty long."

"And look at his feet. They're real big."

"Just the back ones. The front ones are shrimpy."

Sitting back on my heels, I surveyed the circle of curious faces. "Okay. What we have here is a little mouse with a pretty long tail, real big back feet, and shrimpy front feet. What I want to know is—how come?"

"I know." The little redheaded girl gasped with delight and bounced forward. "So he can jump. Just like my brother's bullfrog."

"Good thinking. So we have our hypothesis: that this mouse has big feet so he can jump. Now we have to test our hypothesis. How do we do that?"

To my vast relief, that stumped them. All except my Jessie, who'd been an extremely good sport so far about knowing all the answers and not getting to say a word. I winked at her. "What d'ya think, Jess?"

She grinned. "Put him down and see if he jumps."

The whole class—all twenty-six if you count Mrs. Welton—oohhed and ahhed when Hopalong strutted his stuff, springing three feet to the wastebasket and five feet to the bookcase. As we all tagged after him, I told them about adaptation and predators versus prey, explaining that Hopalong's soaring leaps were his primary defense against the swoop of an owl or the pounce of a wolf.

Next out came Lady, an arctic fox more properly known as *Alopex lagopus*. Even the dullest kid couldn't help noticing that the rich brown fur of her body finished with a stark white tail, and most immediately sensed the nature of her adaptation. The skinny boy was the first to state it in simple terms. "She turns white to match the snow."

I smiled at him. "That's right. Arctic foxes like Lady are just one of the many animals that change colors to match their surroundings. What's another word for changing colors like that?"

I pretended not to notice Jessie rocking back and forth, eager to shine again for Mom. The rest of the bunch was thinking hard about my question. Their faces scrunched up with concentration. One little fellow raised a tentative hand, then snatched it back when I started to call on him. "I'll give you a hint. Changing colors to match their surroundings is very big with guys like G.I. Joe and his pals."

Tentative no longer, the little hand shot up, but the word was out even before his arm reached full extension. "Camo. They put on camo. Just like Lady."

"Right." I grinned. "Camo is short for camouflage.

G.I. Joe paints his face and his clothes and his tank so his enemies can't see him. And Lady's fur turns white so her enemies can't see her. That's another adaptation. Like Hopalong's big jumps."

Mrs. Welton already had Hopalong in the safe circle of her hands. I dragged another chair forward so the boy who knew camo could sit down and hold Lady in his lap. It was time to bring out Esther, our best swimmer and biggest star. Belle Doyon found the river otter in the Kuskokwim Delta, hopelessly snared in a snarl of monofilament line tossed aside by a slob fisherman and near death from starvation. Belle runs trap lines, and at another time of the year she might have killed Esther for her fur, which trappers rate 100 on a scale of 0–100 for durability. But the warm weather singeing of her guard hairs and starvation had combined to temporarily reduce the quality of her pelt, so Belle brought the otter to Nina, instead.

All wild things, including all *Lutra canadensis* like Esther, should live free. However, at one time or another, individual members of almost every species have become so patterned on man that they give up their wild ways. Probably that's how our long-ago ancestors first got started domesticating cats, dogs, horses, pigs, cows, sheep, etc. In any case, such a one is Esther, who adamantly refused to take her chance at freedom during several attempts to release her into the wild. So now, like Nina, she's a part of the family. I even overcame my native dislike of dams long enough to fiddle with the creek running through our property to create a nice deep pool for Esther. The fish she requires come from our local Safeway, where the manager is happy to sell me everything he has that's past its prime. I have a hypothesis that the marked decline in our neighborhood frog population may be due to Esther's desire for fresh kills and a need to hone her hunting skills, but the research on that isn't yet complete.

She was a big hit with the kids in Mrs. Welton's class. Like her seagoing cousins in Prince William Sound, who suffered so grievously because of America's addiction to oil, Esther turns dark eyes filled with curiosity and a twitching, bewhiskered nose on the world and finds it delightful. She loves to slide down muddy slopes in summer and snowbanks in winter, alternating between basic bellyflops and a more ambitious luge-like technique on her back that involves steering with her long tapered tail. Laughter pealed at those stories as the children came up to meet her, inquisitive fingers gently exploring her four webbed feet and softly stroking the thick gray fur of her throat. Where Hopalong is skittish and Lady stiff, Esther is all sleek solemnity and frank inquiry. As a rule, the fuzzy-wuzzy and cuddly approach to wildlife pisses me off, but I have to admit that getting to know Esther sometimes makes me wonder. I'm certainly not among those who think we could talk to the whales if only we knew their language. On the other hand, the idea that all of earth's creatures, with the exception of man, are just dumb animals is also nonsense. If you don't believe me, you should meet Esther.

All in all, it'd been a pretty good day. When the dismissal bell rang, Mrs. Welton organized her troops for going home while Jessie helped me get the animals back in their pet carriers. We carried them out to the 4-Runner and loaded them in. That's when I started wondering where Jake was. For one year only he and

Jessie go to the same school, a school where fifth grade and first grade dismiss at the same time. I'd started muttering as I unlocked the door, and when I climbed behind the wheel, Jess sighed, rolled her eyes, and called me Mom in that two-syllable way that means "how dumb."

I craned my head around, scanning for Jake. "What is it, sweetie?"

"Jake's not here, Mama."

I turned back to her. "He's not?"

Another sigh. "No. Don't you remember? He had that airplane thing today." She waved a vague hand above her head. "He's up there somewhere."

You *can* go hot and cold at the same time, burning with anger and freezing with fear. Jake's love of flying had outlived his father but not my determination to keep him firmly on the ground. Until today. And I knew just who to blame.

When we got to Nina's clinic, I pasted a pleasant smile on my face and breezed past the receptionist with a hearty "Hi, Dave." My housemate and friend was in the laboratory at the back of the building, face scrunched over the eyepiece of a microscope.

She must have heard me coming because she pushed back from the high counter and turned toward me. "Boy, am I glad to see you. The Washington, D.C., office has been calling all afternoon. Your boss arrives in an hour."

That stopped me. "Boyce Reade? Coming here?"

Nina nodded. "And that's not all. They got the grizzly that killed Roland. They're flying it in sometime tonight."

5

Even with his shirt on, Boyce Reade is something to see. The thick mane of dark hair may be too unruly and the rain-gray eyes too amused for masculine perfection, but my boss is definitely a pretty man. As soon as he stepped into Anchorage's international concourse, every boy watcher in the vicinity of the Northwest gate was hooked. And there's more to the Reade fascination than simply good looks, impeccable tailoring, and *noblesse oblige*. Observe the cool flicker glowing deep inside those amused eyes. Note the healthy spring of each yard-eating step. Regard the broad, blunt-fingered hands which promise both power and dexterity. Sometimes I think Boyce Reade may be among the last of a dying breed, a pretty man who is also a manly man—superbly conditioned, vaguely predatory, hale and hearty in an animalistic, life-affirming way. Draped in crisp pinstripes or rumpled corduroys, he looks great either way. Take off the monogrammed shirt, and he looks even better.

I found that out after we got to his tenth-floor room in Tower III of the Hotel Captain Cook less than an hour after his flight from Hong Kong landed. No checked baggage for Boyce Reade. A seasoned world traveler since he toddled, he emerged from the gangway with a battered knapsack slung over one shoulder and a folded garment bag over the other and beelined for the parking lot. I trotted ahead, silently reproving myself for even bothering to check the 4-Runner. How come even the briefest stay in short-term parking requires a ransom worthy of Ali Baba and the Forty Thieves?

Boyce came up beside me as I unlocked the passenger door. He swung his baggage into the back seat and grinned down at me. "Remember the first question you asked after the *Exxon Valdez* ran aground?"

A blush flashed over my face, burning my cheeks and throat before I had a chance to turn away. Instead, I lifted my chin. "If you'd rather I fly everywhere I have to go, just say the word."

As his grin faded into a small half-smile, Boyce gently cupped my chin. "I can give you the exact words. 'How much of your personal portfolio is in fossil fuels?' *Zap!* That one struck home, I must say."

I took a step back, pulling free of his hand. "Yeah. Well, now it's your turn." I shrugged as I circled the hood and opened my door. "If I'm lucky, the V-6 gives me twenty miles per gallon on the highway. As far as four-wheeling goes, I don't even want think about fuel efficiency."

Boyce climbed into the other bucket seat and fiddled with the shoulder belt. "Neither does Congress, which is why I came. Looks like the push for renewed oil exploration up here is no longer either

Bristol Bay or the Arctic National Wildlife Refuge. The drillers want to open up both as soon as possible. And Congress may be in a mood to agree."

I handed the booth attendant a five and got even less change than I'd expected. "Damn those fools and their deficit, too."

Question: What does oil exploration in Alaska have to do with the federal deficit? Answer: Plenty. Of money, that is. Maybe even more than the $25.8 billion—yes, *billion*—in federal taxes paid through 1987 by the companies that own the existing North Slope oil fields. That kind of money buys lots of friends in Washington, D.C., these days. And although big oil whines about high taxes and the burden of $100,000 a day drilling costs, don't get out your handkerchiefs just yet. By 1987 they'd racked up an after-tax profit of $42.6 billion—yes, *billion*—on their investment, which works out to a 44 percent profit. Put it another way: $6 in profit on each of the two million barrels of oil that flow south from Prudhoe Bay to Valdez each day equals a *daily* profit of $12 million. With economics like that, how much chance do you think there is that any of the last pristine remnants of wild America will stay derrick-free?

Bitter realities like that are enough to silence even the most eternal optimist, so I didn't have much to say on the drive to the hotel. Boyce filled me in on his latest around-the-world jaunt—a series of how-to seminars for fledgling environmental groups in the budding democracies of Eastern Europe, giving a group of Middle Eastern sheiks the bad news of our assessment of lasting environmental consequences from the 1991 Persian Gulf war, and negotiating further subsidies with the communist mandarins in Peking to ensure the continued survival of Great Pandas in the wild. Not exactly the tasks you'd expect to see listed in the job description for the executive director of the Wild America Society, but lately times have changed. For the worse. We've gone global because the problems have.

After checking in with the Captain Cook's front desk, Boyce offered me a drink, and I dutifully followed him into an Up elevator. The door had already opened to the tenth floor before I realized we were not heading for the rooftop lounge at the Crow's Nest. He held the door to his room for me before dumping his gear on the queen-size bed, grabbing the ice bucket from the bathroom, and promising to "be right back" as he disappeared down the corridor. I gave about a second's thought to kicking off my shoes and curling up on one end of the couch before deciding the familiar view of the Cook Inlet mudflats was too compelling to be overlooked. When Boyce rattled back in with a bucket of hollow ice, I was studying the framed nautical chart hanging near the bathroom door.

"What'll you have—Scotch or vodka?" He snagged a nifty leather box out of his knapsack and opened it, displaying two engraved silver flasks and matching jiggers. "My Arabian survival kit. Don't leave home without it."

With a drink in my hand, I no longer felt awkward. False courage, perhaps, and not real smart for a lady who once had a problem getting the cork back in the bottle, but there it is. Boyce certainly helped things along by turning his attention to domestic duties. He hung the garment bag in the closet before pulling out the hangers one by one, giving the contents a brisk shake and placing each along the rod. Next he dug his personal kit out of his knapsack and arranged the bathroom to his liking. Finally he stacked a fat paperback thriller atop a thinner series mystery on the bedside table and then propped the queen-size pillows against the headboard and stretched out on the bed.

By that time I'd found the cozy end of the couch. I smiled and raised my glass in his direction. "Home?"

He took a respectable swallow and nodded. "Home. And how about yours? Kids okay?"

For the length of one drink, we caught each other up on the personal sides of our lives, swapping kid stories and woes. His two are older than mine and, I think, more pressured. The girl had an ulcer by the age of fourteen and her younger brother has been in counseling for two years. City living does that to you. So does being born into the tenth generation of America's WASP aristocracy, with a string of three-named ancestors to live up to even though the family's had it made for 125 years. Boyce also has a wife named Eleanor, but he never mentions her. I saw her picture once in the back of a slick magazine that features black-and-white snapshots of society parties and charity balls. Eleanor Bristow Reade had the look of icy elegance— blond, beautiful, and brittle. Maybe that's sour grapes on my part. Growing up is hard enough without being a brunette in an age where "blondes have more fun." But you have to wonder about a woman whose husband has never mentioned her—not once!—in the four years I've worked for him.

Boyce drained his glass and swung his feet to the

floor. "Mind if I grab a shower before taking you out to dinner?" He checked the watch strapped to his left wrist. "We have six-thirty reservations at the Marx Bros. Café."

I mumbled agreement and just kept babbling as he moved around the room, pulling the tie from his collar, flipping his cordovan loafers into the closet, selecting pieces of clothing from the pockets of his garment bag, unbuttoning his shirt. None of which was deliberately provocative, mind you. Blame my white-bread, middle-class background for that—nice girls just don't hang out in a man's hotel room while he's having a bath. And I'll admit to feeling lots of little zings deep inside whenever my boss is around. I'm a biologist, after all, and he's a magnificent specimen.

Somehow I'd gotten around to my trip to McNeil River. Boyce had moved into the bathroom, leaving the door cracked as I prattled on, edging ever closer to hysteria. "So that's when I found him. Roland, I mean."

I whuffed, like a grizzly in distress. "He was the k-k-kill."

Boyce nudged open the door with a naked elbow and stepped back into the room, still in pants but stripped above the waist. "My God, Lauren." He wrestled his arms free of the white T-shirt strung bicep to bicep across his bare chest. "It must have been ghastly. You poor girl."

He crossed the room and knelt before me, taking my hands in his. "The summer after I married, I went sailing with my brother-in-law, Tad Bristow. He was also my best friend." His fingers tightened around mine. "The jib got away from me and the boom broke his neck, killing him instantly. And amid all the shock and horror, what I felt most strongly in that instant was relief that it was him and not me."

I tried to draw my hands away, but he held on. "And in the next instant my relief was overwhelmed by guilt. Because I was glad to be alive. Because I was glad I had not died."

He looked at me with those glowing gray eyes, a magnificent animal inside that firmly muscled pelt, all coiled energy and native grace. A fine example, too, of those characteristics that set our species apart from most others—compassion, understanding, and a willingness to help me admit that part of my reaction to Roland's death which couldn't be borne. I blinked back tears. "The pilot who flew me out said it should have been me."

He sighed and shook his head. "And you believed him. Oh, not in the conscious part of your mind or your heart, maybe." He laid a hand along the side of my head. "But somewhere darker. Way down deep where everything's reduced to the basics, the fundamentals. The same dark and deep place that was the origin of that instant surge of relief that the bear killed your friend instead of you."

For the longest time I just looked at him, in awe of his beauty and his insight. Finally I ducked free of his hand and gave him my most confident smile. "I think you're right, Boyce. And I think it's going to be better now. Thank you."

He nodded without speaking and stalked back to the bathroom, shutting the door firmly behind him and leaving me with the feeling of having taken another great leap in the curious intimacy we'd shared from the moment of our meeting. Not that I could ever claim to understand Boyce Reade. Not yet, anyway. He'd been a mystery to me right from the start, right from the day he called up with no warning and offered me the job that was the other half to saving my sanity after Max died. I'd heard of him, of course, but I still thought the phone call was a put-on. The Wild America Society had never in its long and distinguished history employed an investigator, and nothing else about Boyce Reade's prodigal return as the grandson of the founding director indicated a change of philosophy.

From my perspective, the main-line conservation group looked like a bunch of guilty third-generation natural resource exploiters trying to make up for Granddaddy's original sins. It seemed to me that what started as a good-old boy network of shared values keyed around preservation through national parks hadn't progressed much in seventy-five years. That's what I told Boyce Reade that first day, and he came right back at me, insisting that times had changed. The combination of America's exploding population, increased leisure spent mostly on the road, and fast-diminishing natural resources meant that the end of the frontier was finally in sight. At hand, in fact, which was why even the most conservative members of the Wild America Society now believed the group needed to do their own science. I'm betting that Vietnam and Watergate and Iran-Contra also had a hand in changing their minds, but Boyce didn't say so. What he did say—a generous salary, adequate expense account, and top-of-the-line facilities—quickly convinced me that he was serious, so I took the job. The latest details of which we spent the next three hours discussing over Dungeness crab ravioli with lemon-basil sauce and grilled scallops with saffron risotto at the Marx Bros. Café.

By the time our waiter brought out the cheesecake and coffee, I had my marching orders: review the current literature dealing with arctic oil spills for anything and everything that could derail Big Oil's latest Alaska land grab and fashion those facts into the kind of testimony Boyce Reade needed to persuade a greedy Congress and fickle public of the folly of America's oil-guzzling ways. Sure thing, and for an encore I promise to preserve truth, beauty, and the American way of life or die trying.

Later, after I traded a quick kiss with Boyce and dropped him outside his hotel, I finally remembered some of what preceded Nina's surprise announcement of my boss's arrival. Like my son Jake's mysterious disappearance from school and Jessie's conviction that he was "up there somewhere." I had the half hour it took to drive home to work myself up again. I suppose my encounter session with Boyce left me too emotionally wrung out to do any kind of a job, because I'd hardly gotten past simmer by the time I opened my front door in Eagle River.

After kicking off my heels and hanging up my blazer, I went looking for Nina and found her in the den, staring as if in a trance at the hype that masquerades as news on CNN. I hiked a hip onto the arm of a wing chair and folded my arms. "So, housemate of mine, what's your explanation?"

She looked up, her cheeks grooved by a deep frown.

"I'm not sure I have one, really. Not for someone with his experience. He had to know that shooting to kill was the only thing that could save him."

A vise clamped down on my lungs, and my words came out in a hiss. "What are you talking about?"

Nina's eyes widened. "Roland Taft. Knowing the grizzly's ferocity, he couldn't be a sentimentalist. So he must have been an extremely poor shot. The wound in the foot only maddened the bear." She spread her hands. "Poor man. One chance to save his life and he missed."

6

Up until Nina told me that Roland had been killed by a brown bear that was wounded, I'd put his death down as a simple case of statistical inevitability. A certain number of grizzly-human interactions will result in maulings, a subset of which will result in death. Tedious but true. Factor in an injury to the bear, and the statistics get much more grim for the human in the scenario. Contrary to popular belief, bears in general and grizzlies in particular *are* predictable—when confronted with a human, most bears choose to skedaddle. The big exception is a sow with cubs, especially if a human somehow gets between Mama and her babies. Grizzly predictability at McNeil River is particularly renowned because over the years many hundreds of tourists have watched brown bears fishing for salmon at the falls without one injury to a human. At times bears at the game sanctuary pass within a yard of humans without even a second glance. The grizzlies at McNeil River are habituated to humans, meaning they don't react with the usual skedaddle because they've learned that the people at McNeil River pose no threat. Which is why Roland Taft never carried a gun. I knew that because he'd told me so. More than once.

"A gun can get you in trouble in bear country," he told me one night a few months after Max's death. "Coming up on one suddenly with a gun in your hand could bring on an attack. That's a fact."

Word of Max's disappearance had finally filtered deep enough into the bush to reach Roland, and he'd made his way to Eagle River to pay his respects. My usual source of wildwood wisdom was Belle Doyon, but I couldn't resist probing for the hypothesis and proof behind Roland's latest fact. I cocked an eyebrow in his direction. "How do you figure?"

He shrugged. "Learning. Few close calls with hunters, a smart bear learns what he needs to look out for is the gun, not the man."

After years of failing to discredit Roland's most outlandish theories, I knew better than to howl at this one. The man's a scientist, after all, and generally has evidence for his conclusions. I invited him to elaborate on the brown bear's ability to learn and leaned forward, ready to the fill in the blanks sometimes left by Roland's choppy pattern of speech.

"First time I saw it's in an adolescent male." His lapis eyes went neon at the memory. "Zonker's so scared when the omega male shows up behind him, he jumps in. Floats on down through the whitewater and ends up in a kind of eddy behind a big rock. Bonk. A big old salmon—dead—floats right into his snout, and Zonker chows down. Then he gets to thinking."

Roland smiled and shook his head. "Just like the lightbulbs in comic books, you know? Right off he starts working on his technique. Hanging out behind that rock, trying it head up, trying it head underwater. Getting it down perfect. Next thing you know Zonker's got an audience—a female named Loulabelle. Couple days later, she's using all his moves. Learned behavior. That's a fact."

At the memory of Roland's certainty, my eyes teared and I slid into the seat of the wing chair, shaking my head. "I don't believe it. Roland never carried a gun. And even if he did, he'd never shoot a bear at McNeil River. Those grizzlies knew him."

Nina aimed the remote at the TV and clicked off CNN. "What makes you so certain?"

I sighed. "He told me." Doubt flashed through her eyes, and I edged forward on the chair. "Remember that day float we took last summer?"

Nina's pale cheeks filled with color. Like all good Alaskans faced with a temperature above seventy and no mosquitoes in sight, Roland had stripped to his shorts on our river trip. During which I caught my lesbian housemate ogling his pectoral display. The garbled explanation Nina offered later comparing her reaction to Roland with her appreciation for Michelangelo's David, I answered with a snort of derision. Say what you like, I think there's a pretty fine line separating interest and desire. And that, Nina said, just shows that deep down I believe that female homosexuality is some kind of disease that can be cured by the right man.

"Where do you think he got that set of pects, anyway?" I spread my opened arms but didn't give her a chance to answer. "He got those pects climbing ropes. Every day. Honing his survival skills against the chance, however unlikely, that he might someday need to shinny up a tree to save his life. Does that sound like the kind of guy who'd shoot a bear he probably knew inside a game sanctuary whose purpose he respected?"

Nina blinked but held her ground, less impressed with my facts than with my vehemence. "I have no reason to doubt anything you say, Lauren. But how do you explain the fresh bullet wound in the bear? Or the gun found with Roland's body?"

A frisson of foreboding ran down my spine. "A gun? What kind of gun? I didn't see any gun."

Nina bent her head against one hand. "I have no idea what kind of gun." She looked up. "I do have the bullet. At the clinic. And most of the bear—a mature boar weighing a little over nine hundred pounds, age probably fifteen, heavily scarred but in quite good health. Except for a minor wound to the left hind foot."

"Great, great, but what about the gun? You said it was found *with* Roland's body." I clasped my hands to keep them from flying around and leaned toward her. "What did you mean?"

"Nothing, really." Nina tossed her head but tried for patience in her tone of voice. "Except for the bear, I don't know any of this myself. I'm telling you what I heard. When ADF&G dropped off the carcass, the driver said, 'Make sure you get the bullet from the hind paw, too. They found the gun with the body.'"

I frowned. "The bullet from the hind paw, too? What's that supposed to mean? There were other bullets?"

"Hello. Are you awake in there?" Nina waved a

hand in front of my face. "ADF&G certainly didn't kill the grizzly with kindness."

I've never been a hunter. I've never taken aim at a living creature. But you can't grow up in our culture without experiencing some slaughter through movies and TV. In the next instant those manufactured memories provided me with a vivid epiphany of the grizzly's destruction—a light wind rippling through the greening sedges on the Mikfik flats and the brown bear grazing without concern at the approach of humans because he'd learned that man was no threat in this place. And then the *crack-crack-crack* of the rifles. Fierce satisfaction welled up inside me, a savage twin to the horrifying relief that Boyce Reade had coaxed me to admit. Call it vengeance or call it retribution—sometimes I think that need to even up the score is at the very heart of our humanity. Observers of the natural world soon learn that in nature indifference reigns supreme. Humans are capable of caring deeply, and I was glad that the bear which killed Roland had been destroyed.

"Mom?" The uncertainty in my son's voice was matched by Jake's hesitant footsteps on the staircase. "Is that you?"

I ducked my head around the wing of the chair until I could see him on the stairs, framed by the doorway to the hall. "I'm home, baby. Get back to bed and I'll be up in a sec to tuck you in."

As soon as he vanished up the stairs, Nina bushwhacked me again. "I told them about Roland." I stiffened. "I had to, Lauren, before they saw it in the paper or on TV."

Suddenly it was all too much—Roland's death, Boyce's revelation, Jake's flying—and I lashed out.

"*You* had to? Is that why Jake went flying today—because *you* decided he could? By what right do *you* make the decisions about my children?"

Even before I'd finished, even before I saw the glint of tears in Nina's eyes, I wanted to swallow those hateful words. She moved with a slow dignity, getting to her feet and gathering up her things before heading out of the den. In the doorway she stopped, framed as my son had been. "Jake didn't fly today. He did spend the afternoon with Travis MacDonald doing something for Civil Air Patrol, but he did not fly."

My kids and I sometimes rewind and start over. When one of us yells "Erase! Erase!" we all back up to our previous position, take a ten count, and try again. Quite often all we need to work things out is a second chance. But life doesn't always work out neatly, and sometimes second chances are hard to come by. There are times when pain can't be avoided, and this was one of them. I listened while Nina made her way through the dining room and kitchen to the suite we'd added for her when she became a permanent part of the family, and then I went upstairs to see my son.

Jake has always been a hard kid to raise because the energy of an entire Little League team is packed into his string-bean body. We're not just talking high energy here. We're talking megawatts. Most adults who've spent any time with my son finally get around to asking if he ever slows down. The answer is no. Jake is either sleeping or GO-GO-GO. Although at my weariest I've doubted my stamina for the job of mothering a megawatt kid, I've never doubted the reward. My son is not one of the bored and sophisticated dullards who pass for kids these days. This is a boy who can get so excited that he loses the power of speech. This is a boy who is transported to tears when a cruel fate befalls a favorite character in an adventure novel. This is a boy who at age eleven shows more understanding of the human heart than most forty-year-olds I know.

In some ways Jake hasn't recovered from losing his dad and probably never will, but I'm positive my son's going to make it. The reason for my optimism is named Travis MacDonald. Trav used to jockey jets off of aircraft carriers and now gets his hours in by flying for the Civil Air Patrol out of Elmendorf Air Force Base. In the search for Max's plane, he was the first pilot up and the last down. We talked on the telephone every day, and after it was all over, Trav stopped by the house to offer his condolences, saw me heading for trouble, and hung around to make sure my kids came through all right. He's an old-fashioned can-do type of guy with an independent streak as wide as the Yukon. He hates credit cards, time clocks, sermons, mortgages, political parties, television, and progress. He lives on fifty acres up near Eklutna in a cabin that features the biggest bathtub I've ever seen and spends most of his time on two of his three grand passions—flying and jazz. What's left he spends on the third—my son—who couldn't find a better guy to teach him how to be a man unless his own father came back to life.

When I got to Jake's room, I found him in his usual post-bedtime mode—cat curled up to the right, drawing gear spread out on the left and my boy sprawled in the middle with his nose buried in a book. I leaned against the doorframe and addressed myself to the upraised cover of what looked like another adventure. "What's the book, bud?"

"The Iceberg Hermit. It's about this kid. He gets shipwrecked. Like in Greenland." Jake stuck a finger in the book and lowered it to his chest. "And he kills this polar bear. But then he finds out she's a mother. So he takes care of the cub. And it's true, Mom. It really happened. In like . . ." He flipped through the pages to the beginning of the book. " . . . like . . . like—here it is—it happened in 1757."

I scooped up the drawing gear and added it to the pile heaped up on his bedside table before sitting down beside him on the bed. "Did he get rescued?"

"I haven't got that far." His eyes brightened. "But he had to. Or else how would anyone know the story? Right?"

"I guess so." I found Jake's alarm clock among the mess on the table and turned up the digital face so he could see it. "Past your bedtime. Way past."

He dropped the book on the floor and yawned, snuggling deeper into his bed. I smoothed the covers across his shoulders. He sighed and laid his cheek against my hand. "Mom? Is it true about your friend, Roland?"

I laid my other hand on his head, fingering hair like silk. "It's true, Jake. He was killed by a bear."

"How did it . . ." He rolled his head until his face was buried in the pillow and his voice muffled. "What was it . . ."

Grisly images flashed through my mind—greening sedges stained the color of rust, a circle of bloody bits—but I edited my memories for Jake's consumption because the nightmare is in the details. "It happened very quickly. A grizzly can take down a moose with one swipe of a paw. And he attacked from fear, not hunger."

46

The silence drew out, long enough for more questions. When none came, I asked one of my own. "Did you have a nice time with Travis today?"

"I guess." Jake rubbed his cheek against my hand. "It was kind of boring. We had to drive all around looking at planes."

"How come?" His eyes fluttered and I lowered my voice. "Is Travis going to buy another plane?"

"I don't think so. See, they're looking for this one plane. For this one pilot." He yawned hugely. "He had a near miss the other day. Second one. So they want the guy bad. Think it's a Cessna, but it could be a . . ."

Even before Jake's voice trailed away, I wasn't paying close attention. Foremost in my mind was the question of how to apologize to Nina. And when. My son's fascination with airplanes was something I couldn't share. Not after Max's death. A few weeks later I was heartily sorry for having tuned out the specifics in Jake's explanation. Never before had I needed to rewind and start over as badly as I did then. On that day I realized that if I'd listened more carefully to Jake, I might have been able to prevent the loss of a human life. My own.

7

Most members of the Smokey the Bear generation express surprise upon learning that our Forest Service no longer consists of happy campers who spend their days building trails but also harbors rabid resource exploiters eager to mow down the last of our ancient forests to harvest logs for export to Japanese chopstick factories. Blame a doctrine called "multiple use" for the contradiction. Multiple use promises all things to all people and fits right in with our nation's philosophy of having it all—trees for loggers *and* trees for habitat, water for irrigation *and* water for fish, development *and* conservation, infinite growth *and* finite resources. The idea also produces some very strange bedfellows at natural resource agencies in this country and explains how I wound up with a pal as unlikely as Vanessa Larrabee.

Vanessa started working for Alaska Fish and Game around the time I did, meaning both of us faced the double whammy of being women and scientists in a department historically run by self-taught men. Talk about resentment! If the only possibility of female company in that place had been Imelda Marcos, I would have polished up the toes of my pumps and set out to befriend her. Despite big hair, vivid fingernails, and the conservative politics of a classic land raper, Vanessa Larrabee turned out to be okay. Texans are like that. Must be something in their flat and dusty native soil that imparts a special zest for life. The best of their women are very sharp, very flirty, and very funny. Vanessa is all three, plus a very competent geologist who specializes in sorting fact from fiction when mining needs threaten critical fish or game habitat.

A couple of days after Boyce Reade's visit, I asked her to meet me for lunch. The vague uneasiness I'd felt ever since Nina mentioned the gun found near Roland's body just wasn't going away. I figured Vanessa would know everything I didn't about the investigation into his death. She promised to meet me at Earthquake Park at twelve-thirty if I'd provide a chef salad, ranch dressing, and iced tea. I wondered why.

"Don't be dense, sugar." Her outrageous nails clicked against the handset. "I'm on a diet."

"Not the menu—the place. Why Earthquake Park? Feeling nostalgic for some good old rock and roll?"

She gave me a sample of the husky laughter that drives men crazy. "'Cause nobody goes there except tourists from Outside. You think I want to be seen consorting with a tree-hugging radical like you? Make that lo-cal ranch, will you, sugar?"

The salad bar at Safeway's superstore on Northern Lights Boulevard featured quarts of the stuff, so I loaded up before heading to the park overlooking the

Knik Arm. What used to be a nice neighborhood was turned into Earthquake Park after some of the expensive homes slid into the sea when the 8.4 rocker struck just before supper on Good Friday 1964. Other parts of Alaska's southern coast had it much worse. I steered clear of the pavilion featuring photos of what was left of the village of Chenega after a ninety-foot tidal wave roared through Prince William Sound, drowning a third of the population. Since the *Exxon Valdez,* Alaskans don't want to be reminded of the near-total destruction at harbors on the same coast where the oil terminal is now located. We also prefer to ignore the pavilion's geological diagrams describing the inevitability of unstable clays shaking into liquid during an earthquake, just as we ignored those facts by choosing to rebuild our city on the ruined foundations of the one that collapsed in 1964. The only Alaskan I know who has actually prepared for the next Big One by stockpiling batteries, water, and canned foods is Vanessa Larrabee. But, then, she *is* a geologist.

I found Miss Safety First on a bench facing the water, searching the clouds banked on the northern horizon for a glimpse of Mt. McKinley. The gauzy pink scarf protecting her hair from stray breezes complemented the lace in the peekaboo cutouts of her tight denim dress, another in this year's Frederick's-of-Hollywood-Goes-West motif.

"Damn that Denali for hiding all the time." She gave a little snort when I sat down next to her. "Though I do suppose we'd mostly stop looking if the mountain showed itself more often. Just like our mamas used to say—nobody appreciates what comes easy or often."

"Maybe your mama said that, but mine didn't." I pulled a clear plastic box of salad out of my canvas shopping bag and passed it to her. "Her only attempt at explaining the facts of life was leaving a book on my bed. *Your Body Is Changing*. A real page-turner."

Vanessa sighed in sympathy as she arranged the salad and paper napkins on her lap. "For all her preaching about lady dos and don'ts, in practice my mama was a good old girl." She drizzled the ranch dressing over her greens. "I spent my childhood kind of confused."

"Is that why you went into rocks?" I busied myself stripping paper off the plastic straws and getting them into the iced teas. "Thought you'd find certainty in science?"

Vanessa's fork stopped halfway to her open mouth. "You do beat all, Lauren." Her eyes went dreamy and she lowered her fork. "I believe you may be right. What I like about geology's the same thing I liked about keeping the books at Mama's dress shop. Once you tote up a column of numbers, you have the answer. No matter how you switch those numbers around, the sum always stays the same."

She flashed me a quick smile. "Same thing with rocks. There's lots of different kinds, but once you've sorted out what's what, you've got the answer. And it never changes. Igneous is igneous, sedimentary is sedimentary, metamorphic is metamorphic."

She settled back against the bench and started eating. But after only two bites, she stopped again, frowning now. "Except that's not strictly true. Rocks do change. Igneous erodes and gets laid down as sediment. And turns metamorphic by getting blown out of a volcano or squeezed between two plates."

I grinned at her. "Ah, that's science for you. The uncertainty lasts forever."

The sun warmed my face as we ate in companionable silence, the length of our friendship ensuring that both of us knew better than to let chatter interfere with the more important business of lunch. Meals should be taken out of doors. Eating is a sensual pleasure, and stimulating the other senses enhances the experience. Food simply tastes better when eyes feast on natural beauty and arms caress soft air. How else do you explain the rhapsodies of backpackers fresh from the trail who've been hiking their butts off and existing on dehydrated glop for weeks?

Vanessa had a ready answer. "Same reason people who won't touch caffeine at home just love the cowboy coffee I brew in camp. Out there folks'll drink—or eat—just about anything, so long as it's hot."

She was right. Human beings, like grizzly bears, are omnivores. Under the right circumstances, anything that can be swallowed is deemed edible. Which is how we finally got around to Roland Taft. To a griz, John Muir said, everything but granite is food. Roland *knew* that. What puzzled me was how a man with his knowledge and experience could screw up badly enough to get killed.

Vanessa patted my forearm. "He was your friend, wasn't he?"

I nodded, not quite trusting my voice. Losing Max had taught me that dams holding back grief sometimes dissolve with breathtaking speed. When my throat stopped quivering, I managed a question. "I wondered what people at ADF&G were saying about what happened?"

"Not much." Vanessa gave another little snort. "Nobody's got the guts to have an opinion anymore. Not with Machine-gun Kirby running things."

My mouth hung open so far only an idiot could mistake the surprise. For her part, Vanessa chuckled. Good old gals from Texas just love surprising people. "Where you been, sugar? Juneau put him in charge of bear country months ago."

I stammered a bit. "Kirby Rogers? They put him in charge? That maniac?"

"Maniac? I wonder." She arched one carefully plucked eyebrow. "He *is* a fine-looking man."

"Vanessa!" I admit to squealing at her tendency to sometimes let hormones get the better of her. "The man's a helo-hunter. And he uses automatic weapons!"

Regret tinged her deep sigh. "There is that. And he did pick a mousy little thing for his number two. You must know her. Name like Frenchette or Blanchette? Something like that." She shivered and tightened the scarf knotted under her chin. "Seems to me there's something awful creepy about that woman."

For creepy, you couldn't beat Kirby Rogers. Not that I'd ever worked with him at ADF&G or come up against him since joining Wild America. Frankly, I'd never even met the guy, but when the wolves story broke a year or two earlier, everybody in Alaska learned of his monstrous legend. When Vanessa rattled on about Rogers's awful assistant, I ignored her to concentrate on scanning my memory for every damning tidbit about the man himself.

Kirby Rogers was a white native, the son of third-generation homesteaders who'd carved their piece of heaven out of the rugged Yukon country near Eagle, hard by the Canadian border. He knew his woodcraft —traplines, fish wheels, dog teams, snowshoes—and had also mastered the essential skills introduced by the white man—mining, bulldozers, snow machines, airplanes. He understood subsistence needs because he'd lived the life. He knew the autumn tasks of getting in wood and taking a moose. He'd spent short winter days checking his traplines and long winter nights curing his furs. He'd gloried in the twin summer gifts of salmon to feed a man's dogs and gold to feed his fantasies. To the Déné, Kirby Rogers was a brother who'd never been barred by the invisible line that kept natives in one end of the village and whites in the other. To sportsmen, Kirby Rogers was the great white hunter, able to do anything natives could and often better. To environmentalists, Kirby Rogers was a nightmare, marrying the native skills of harvesting the wild with the white man's capacity for excess.

At Alaska Fish and Game, Kirby Rogers had always been controversial. Critical reviews greeted his debut when he served on the caribou team for the pipeline studies. Even before the completion of the necessary research, Rogers proclaimed that animals and industry could coexist. That certainty earned him accusations of favoring big oil and North Slope development at any cost. Not long after, the subject was a proposal to prohibit foreign fishing within two hundred miles of the American coast. Although the final decision lay with the federal government, Kirby Rogers weighed in anyway, expressing outrage that Americans would turn away from such founding principles as free trade and freedom of the seas. That performance earned him the reputation of favoring foreigners who wanted to factory-fish in Prince William Sound. The capstone achievement that elevated him to legend came from his penchant for equipping himself with automatic weapons and a helicopter when culling wolf packs.

Find the sport in a hunt that consists of stalking the pack from the air, giving chase until the wolves finally hold their ground from sheer exhaustion, then landing the machine and killing every animal in sight with a burst from a machine gun. That's legal in Alaska. At least for wolves. Other species are "protected" by regulations requiring that the landing and the shooting can't happen on the same day, but the Wild American Society figures 75 percent of the grizzly bears taken each year are shot from the air anyway. The ranks of slob hunters grow yearly and aerial hunts represent the worst of the worst. Is it any wonder that, despite official sanction, helo-hunting earned Kirby Rogers the title Saddam of the North?

Ever a sucker for a pretty face, Vanessa objected when I repeated the nickname. "I really don't think that's fair, Lauren. He's not that nasty." Her eyes danced with laughter. "I like 'Machine-gun Kirby' myself."

"Being from Texas, you would. You're all gun nuts down there." I leaned back against the bench, stretching my legs out full and crossing my ankles. "How's his science?"

"Kinda shaky, from what I hear. Not that he does much. Infrequent publication and sloppy statistics—the usual complaint. He had a paper out a few months ago that really set off some howls. About bears, I think."

I stiffened and turned toward her in time to see her

eyes go cloudy. She warned me off speaking by raising a hand. "Hold on a second. Bears. Brown bears. Yup, down at McNeil River."

Memory's a funny thing. Vanessa revived hers by repeating key words and seeing what popped into her mind. "Aggressive behavior. Factors in predicting."

The clouds cleared from her eyes, and she gave me a triumphant smile. "'Factors in predicting aggressive behavior in Alaskan brown bears at the McNeil River Game Sanctuary.' By Kirby Rogers."

"And you said there was a beef about it?" I cocked my head. "Somebody wrote a rebuttal?"

"I'll say." Vanessa nodded slowly. "Just about called old Kirby a liar."

Scientists can get pretty passionate in defense of their positions, but libel is still kind of unusual. I spread my hands. "I wonder who it was?"

"I remember that, too." Vanessa didn't bother scrunching up her eyes this time, so I had no time to prepare for the shocker she delivered next. "Your friend, that's who."

This time her smile looked sick. "It was Roland Taft called Kirby Rogers a liar."

8

Lunch with Vanessa took more time than I'd allotted, forcing me to spend the rest of the afternoon running at full-tilt boogie. Some days the schedule is just too full for comfort. I'd spent the morning cruising the offices of every natural resource agency in Anchorage, buttonholing bureaucrats in hopes of uncovering some wondrous bit of new data that would magically prevent Big Oil from raping the Artic National Wildlife Refuge. Not that I expected to find anything. That seemed about as likely as surfing the Beaufort Sea. Any federal or state bureaucrat worth his civil service rating would have long ago deep-sixed data that explosive. Some might consider lunching with a geologist yet another example of my perseverance in defense of the wild, but they would be mistaken. Vanessa is a Texan, after all, and committed to full development of all extractive industries. I didn't even bother asking. Boyce Reade's need of new ammunition for his upcoming Congressional testimony might have to wait for another day because his ace investigator had run out of time. She had a three o'clock date with her son.

Domestic crises large and small often knock my job from the top spot on my list of priorities, and today was no exception. Somewhere in the mountains near the Alyeska Ski Resort was a worried wolf bitch who'd lost a pup. Closer to home, my oldest pup had developed an attachment to the little critter which threatened our domestic harmony. Jake's unrelenting insistence on keeping the wolf pup finally wavered when I promised to give the notion due consideration if the mother couldn't be found. After further negotiations, I consented to having my son accompany me in the search so he could "make sure you really found her." Another heartwarming example of the unshakable trust that pediatric headshrinkers promise when lines of communication open between parent and child.

Swinging the 4-Runner back onto Northern Lights Boulevard, I headed east toward Alaska Pacific University, intending to dig out a copy of the bear article written by Kirby Rogers and Roland Taft's rebuttal. After locating the General Science Index in the library's reference section, I scanned the most recent updates, finding the citation for Kirby Rogers but no entry for Roland's rebuttal. That turned up in the Periodic Guide, which cited *New Age Naturalist,* a journal I didn't know. The original Rogers article appeared in a publication of the Bear Biology Association, which I easily found and quickly copied. *New Age Naturalist* proved harder to locate. Finally I asked the student clerk manning the reference desk for help.

"New Age Naturalist? Yeah, we've got it." She pointed toward the racks of general interest magazines in the main lobby. "It's over there with all the other mysto-squeezo junk."

The cover of the issue I wanted featured a pen-and-ink drawing depicting a circle of forest creatures dancing around a crystal which hung in midair. I had little time for making copies and even less to spare to puzzle out the meaning of the bizarre cover. Actually reading the articles had to wait, too. I had barely enough time left to scoot north on the Glenn Highway and get to Jake's school in Eagle River before dismissal.

On the way I remembered to pick up the wolf pup at Nina's clinic, so in the end I arrived fifteen minutes late. Even before the truck stopped, my son's irritation was evident in the set of his mouth and shoulders. Rather than smooth things over, I compounded the problem by snapping at him. "You're wearing canvas high-tops? To go hiking?"

"Chill out, will ya?" Jake slumped into the seat, knapsack on his lap. He yanked the zipper open. "I got my hiking boots in here."

That shut me up for about twenty miles. Jake amused himself by running up and down the AM and FM dials on the radio before reaching for the first cassette. The kid's tape style consists of agonizing searches for particular songs. Fast-forward, oops! rewind, darn!—the whole schtick drives me nuts. In self-defense I pulled into the lot of a convenience store just outside Chugach State Park, handed him a five-dollar bill, and urged him to stock up on snacks. By the time he returned—laden with a Dr Pepper, a small bag of sour-cream-and-onion chips, and a large bag of Skittles—the speakers wailed with Gladys Knight, a favorite from way back.

With much smacking of lips, Jake munched happily until we got to the turnoff for Girdwood. At that point he drained his soda, burped softly behind a halfheartedly raised hand, and straightened up. "How we going to find the mother?"

"Good question. I wish I knew the answer." Downshifting, I swung the 4-Runner off the highway. "The way Nina heard it, the pup came *down* the chair lift."

"So maybe we should start by taking him back up?" He raised his eyes to search out the high country. The mountain's elevation is only thirty-nine hundred feet, but with timberline at fifteen hundred feet, there's plenty of bare rock up there. "I didn't think wolves lived up so high."

"They don't always. Wolves prefer tundra and open forests." I nosed the truck into the parking lot outside the main lodge. "Which is why we're going to start by asking a few questions. The hard part is knowing who to ask."

Actually, figuring out who isn't all that hard. Ask the guy who's not too busy to notice what's going on and not too stuffy to get in on the latest gossip. In other words, ask the plebians who do the dirty work. In a restaurant, I'd pick the busboy out front and the dishwasher in the kitchen. The secret is finding the guy whose job doesn't require a lot of brain activity so plenty of room's left for idle curiosity. Of course, sometimes the plebians are too stupid to be curious. On the other hand, our television culture gives every one of us plenty of experience in passive observation. In this case I figured the chair-lift attendants were my best bet. Most of them are ski bums, guys who endure performing a menial, mind-numbing task for forty hours a week because they get to spend the rest of the time skiing for free. I also figured I might get lucky and actually find the one who'd been working the day the wolf pup rode down the chair lift.

Jake stood off by himself, cuddling the wolf, while I made my way over to the husky blond fellow manning Chair I. He traded wisecracks with a knot of tourists, mostly older women with blue hair and huge hand-bags, as he loaded them onto the chair for the trip to the Skyride Restaurant twenty-three hundred feet up the mountain. The soups and sandwiches up there may be standard issue, but the view is out of this world—a bird's eye of Glacier Valley in one direction and the full expanse of Turnagain Arm in the other. When the last chair of tourists cleared the loading platform, I moved in, asking if he'd been on duty the day the wolf pup rode down in the chair.

"No way, lady." He glanced over my shoulder at Jake. "No pets of any kind on the chair lift."

"You don't understand. My mistake." I flashed him my best smile. "My son is holding a wolf pup that someone from Outside found up on the mountain last week and brought down on the chair lift."

I motioned Jake forward, hoping the fellow had the smarts to see that this was no dog pup. "We want to return him to his litter but need some idea of where to start looking."

When Jake stopped beside us, the chair-lift attend-ant reached out a stubby finger and touched the pup's fuzzy head. I smiled again, trying for reassurance. "Were you working the day this little guy rode down on the chair?"

"Huh?" The blond jumped back a ways. "No! Not me." He glanced around quickly, then stepped back into our circle, speaking with a low voice. "I had the day off, but I heard about it. Boy, was management ever pissed. Both guys working the lift that day got sacked. And the one down here had nothing to do with it."

Ever the idealist, Jake piped right up. "Hey, that's not fair. That stinks." He scowled in the direction of the lodge. "What a bunch of geeks."

"You said it. Geeks to the max." The blond nodded, tossing a scowl of his own toward the resort offices. "And not so smart, either." His eyes skittered through another quick surveillance. "There's a guy upstairs knows all about them wolves. A dishwasher named Frankie. He's been feeding them."

My heart dropped into a pit at that bit of news. Wolves don't stand much of a chance in any of Alaska's populated areas. As many as one third of the estimated fifteen thousand wolves in the state are taken by hunters and trappers each year. A pack dependent on handouts from humans was doomed for sure. Especially if the handouts were really bait by a trapper intent on securing his future harvest. But even if that turned out to be true, my Jake still had no right to keep the wolf pup. I looked up the mountain, not relishing the climb. "Is Frankie working today?"

"Oh, sure." The attendant folded his arms. "Lift closes at five, but he don't finish till an hour after that."

I touched my son's arm. "We better get hiking if we're going to get up there in time."

The attendant spread his arms. "Hey, take the chair."

Jake shook his head firmly. "No way. You'd get in trouble."

"Nah." The blond grinned. "This is my last day. I've had enough of this shit. I got a job lined up on a trawler out of Dillingham." He swept a hand toward the chair lining up on the loading platform. "Be my guest."

Up on the mountain Jake stayed out of sight with the pup while I circled the glassed-in restaurant until I found the employees' entrance to the kitchen. The dishwashing station turned out to be right by the door. And Frankie turned out to be a pimply-faced teenager with a very big heart and very few brains. He followed me outside without a moment's hesitation. "What's up?"

I led the way to a beat-up picnic table sheltered by some scrubby spruce as Jake angled in our direction from his vantage point closer to the sun deck. Frankie's eyes lit when he spotted the wolf pup. "Hey, you brought him back. You brought back my wolf."

I used my sternest schoolmarm tone of voice. "Your wolf, Frankie? How do you figure?"

He squared his shoulders. "How? Because I bagged him. Finders keepers."

Ever so gently I nudged Frankie backward until the bench of the picnic table caught him behind the knees and he folded onto the seat. I planted a foot on the bench beside him and leaned my arms across the bent knee. "You caught him, huh? Keep him in a cage?" The boy nodded, less certain of his rights now. "How'd he look in there? A wild thing used to living free."

Frankie mumbled something I couldn't make out. I

touched his shoulder and asked him to say it again. "Not so hot." His voice just cleared a whisper. "He didn't look so hot in a cage."

I nodded at Jake, who handed the pup to Frankie. The dishwasher clutched the wolf against his chest, rubbing his cheek in the soft, deep fur. I leaned closer, speaking softly. "How long have you been feeding the wolves, Frankie?"

He stiffened, no longer comforted by that glorious fur. "What are you talking about? Who are you, anyway?"

I straightened. "I'm a wildlife investigator, Frankie. And I know you've been feeding the wolves."

He looked at me without speaking, eyes blinking rapidly to hold back the tears.

"You know what happens to wolves who get fed?"

He shook his head.

"They end up dead with their pelt decorating the hood of a parka. Because they learn a bad lesson, Frankie. They learn that man is a safe source of food. Which isn't true. For a wolf, the only safety is in fearing men, Frankie. Because man is their enemy."

Sobbing, he buried his face against the pup. "I didn't mean no harm. I don't want him to get hurt."

I dropped onto the bench next to Frankie and swung an arm around his shoulder. "I know you didn't. And he won't. Not if you return him to his den tonight."

Sniffing hard, he wiped a sleeve under his nose and fixed his eyes on some distant spot. I tried to keep anything whiny and self-righteous out of my plea. "Stop leaving them food, Frankie. They'll find plenty on their own. And stay away from them. Let the wolves get their fear back."

That was enough. On pure instinct, I stood up, grabbed Jake by the elbow, and got out of there, leaving Frankie alone on the bench with his wolf. Unfortunately, I headed in the wrong direction, away from the chair lift. Rather than ruining that exit, we headed down the mountain on foot, trying to find the driest route through rotten snow and soggy meadow. Jake's mouth ran the whole time, mostly musing about the chances of Frankie actually returning the pup and marveling at how "cool" I'd been not to yell at the poor kid. Pretending I found the hike more taxing than it actually was, I confined my responses to a series of hmmms and gloried in my son's praises. From pain-in-the-butt nag to his latest hero, all in three hours. Who wouldn't love it?

The glow lasted straight through dinner and on into the evening. Nina rushed off to softball practice, so Jake cleared up the kitchen while I listened to Jessie read. After KP duty, he joined us in my bedroom for another chapter of *Tom Sawyer*. We're reading our way through the great books, and Twain's tale still captivates kids today. Lights out at nine meant I could finally look over the articles I'd copied at the university library earlier in the day.

The article by Kirby Rogers was about what I expected—bunches of tables and charts that looked great but had nothing important to say and even the most obvious conclusions modified into mush in an attempt to remain "objective." Good science is not about playing it safe. Remember Galileo, who spent the last years of his life under house arrest for refusing to renounce his belief that the Earth orbited the Sun? Or how about Charles Darwin? If you think today's bellowing fundamentalists are bad, imagine the vilification endured a hundred-plus years ago by the guy who came up with evolution in the first place. On the face of it, Kirby Rogers had contented himself with bureaucratic science—safety first and the advance of knowledge much, much later.

I turned to Roland's rebuttal with high hopes, eager for him to take the helo-hunter apart. But the letter to *New Age Naturalist* had an unexpected and narrow focus, restricting comment to a one-paragraph appendix in which Rogers speculated on possible factors in predicting aggressive behavior in brown bear-human interactions. One sentence of Roland's rebuttal was especially chilling. *"My conviction that bears are able to learn is the reason I never carry a firearm in grizzly country,"* the dead man wrote. Then how to explain the gun found near his body and the bullet in the paw of the bear that killed him?

9

Sometimes even the best efforts end in failure. So did my earnest attempt to hate Kirby Rogers. The man stood for everything I loathed—helo-hunting, land raping, bureaucratic science. The weight of his words had helped persuade officials to allow construction of the eight-hundred-mile fence of oil that bisects Alaska from Prudhoe Bay to Valdez, a decision that inevitably resulted in the obscenity of eleven million gallons spilled into the pristine waters of Prince William Sound. His opposition to strict controls on drift nets was one reason Asian fishing fleets were still allowed to strip-mine our waters, needlessly killing thousands of dolphins, turtles, and sea birds along with their target catch. His strident defense of aerial hunting effectively atomized a longtime sportsman's taboo, making the idea a fit topic of conversation *and* consideration once again. I walked into the ADF&G building on Raspberry Road confident of the justice of my contempt for the man in charge of bear country. An hour later I wobbled out a quivering mass of doubt and contradictions.

Talk about getting schmoozed! Kirby Rogers made Cary Grant at his most debonair seem about as suave as Pee-wee Herman. A little rough on the edges, maybe, but still a master of self-deprecating charm. I wanted to match him—joust for joust, riposte for riposte—but my best turned out to be hopelessly outclassed. There's a scene in *To Catch a Thief* where Grant's pretending to be a lumber baron from Oregon, and Grace Kelly says, "Where in Oregon? The Rogue River?" No wonder she married royalty! That's the kind of wit I aimed for. What I managed fell somewhere between Bette Midler and Whoopi Goldberg.

The mousy assistant didn't throw me, because Vanessa'd warned me, but his office was a surprise. I searched in vain for the little things I'd expected—the overblown paperweight that screamed ego, the framed hunting prints that cried social climber, the pretentious desk that befitted the power-mad. The desk turned out to be a beat-up metal job with a Daffy Duck coffee mug holding down his paperwork, with a Scotch-taped poster advertising Ansel Adams prints the sole decoration on the wall. Only after I'd failed in my search for damning evidence did I deign to notice the man himself.

Wow!

For once in her life my pal Vanessa had not been exaggerating. Not merely fine-looking—Kirby Rogers was fabulous! A big man with a rugged but handsome face, thick waves of hair the color of freshly churned butter, and a gleam of amusement dancing in his rich brown eyes. He got to his feet and offered his hand across the top of his desk. "Ms. Maxwell. I'm happy to finally have the pleasure. I've heard a lot about you."

One firm, brisk shake and I got to sit down, hoping the false confidence in my voice disguised the weakness of my knees. "Praise, no doubt. I'm a well-known defender of truth, justice, and the American way."

He tossed back his head and laughed long and loud, striking off a spark of gratification deep inside my pounding heart. When his easy laughter trailed off, he leaned forward and anchored his elbows on his desk. "Among other things. Like good science. Loyalty. Loss."

I acknowledged the implication of Max's death with a brief nod and struggled to regain the upper hand I'd never had. "I've heard a fair bit about you, too. The pipeline. Drift nets. Helo-hunting." Nothing—not a blink of surprise or sigh of frustration. "I wonder where you stand on oil exploration of the Arctic Refuge?"

Now he sighed, moving his eyes from mine for the first time since we'd made contact. "I'm standing over on the sidelines, shaking my head with disgust. The Arctic will be opened for exploration, pumped of the little oil they'll find and parts of it damaged beyond repair."

His eyes returned to mine, a glitter of anger marring the previous serenity. "Not that it can't been done right. But nobody'll bother. Southern California will still be one long polluted traffic jam with gas guzzlers reigning supreme."

I blurted out the first thing that came into my head. "But you favored the pipeline."

"Hell, yes. After the first oil embargo, everybody

with any brains had to. We were sitting ducks." He shook his head. "I didn't favor shipping the oil through Prince William Sound, but Congress didn't want to share the wealth by piping it through Canada. And I thought we'd wise up and get a handle on our consumption. I was wrong."

He rested his chin on one upraised hand and turned those big brown eyes on me again. "Drift nets? An incredibly wasteful technology, but outlawing them won't solve the underlying problem of Asians—particularly the Japanese—taking more than their fair share of the ocean's resources. As long as the Japs keep us focused on the technology, we never get around to the real problem."

Good thing he wasn't finished, because I couldn't think of a thing to say. "Helo-hunting?" He raised an eyebrow in my direction. "Come on and admit it. Your horror of the helicopter is just a smokescreen. What you *really* hate is the hunting. There's no such thing as a humane hunt, no way to make killing humane or hunting fair. It's not. And I refuse to pretend it is."

Life's funny. Part of the way we define ourselves is by figuring out who we're *not*. Up until then, one of the main people I happened not to be was Kirby Rogers. Turned out that even though the man was to the right of Genghis Khan, on each point of controversy his decision was made for a valid reason. Emphasis on *reason*. Every case cited against him fell into the gray area of supposition, the kind the media usually hype into fact with stories beginning *"Scientists now believe . . ."* I bet Kirby Rogers hates news stories in that vein, but to me, science isn't about reason or fact or any other empirical conclusion. To me, science is about faith and belief and the great leaps of imagination that led Marie Curie to X rays and Albert Einstein to relativity. In the religion that is science, imagining is God's grace and proving is man's penance. Once the fact is established, you're talking about history, not science. Mirroring the political gulf yawning between us was the difference in scientific philosophy—Kirby Rogers espousing reason and method while I preferred instinct and experiment. But even at my most intolerant, I never could hate a guy just because he disagreed with me. And science needs both doers and dreamers because the tension generated by opposing views is the fuel that advances knowledge.

For that reason, I found myself searching for an appropriate peace offering to smooth over my earlier harshness. The good looks and charm of Kirby Rogers had absolutely nothing to do with my change of heart. I *am* a scientist, after all. I settled on a bit of information I'd picked up from one of those "Ain't Life Strange" fillers printed in magazines and newsletters. "Technology's not the problem. Sometimes technology helps the environment. The automobile did."

That grabbed him. A conservative never expects to hear an environmentalist praising the automobile. Rogers sat back in his chair and smiled. "Okay. I'll bite. How has the automobile helped the environment?"

"By saving millions of acres of forest from clearcutting. Between 1850 and 1910, 190 million acres of forest were cleared for agriculture in this country. That's as much acreage as we have in national forest today." I smiled and spread my hands. "And a third of that cut—62 million acres—was cleared to produce horse feed. The automobile reduced our dependence on horses and took the pressure off the woods."

He turned toward the Ansel Adams poster with the famous shots of Yosemite's Half Dome and a south-western moonrise, and the brightness of his eyes dimmed. "Bit by bit, it's slipping away. In another hundred years all the wild places will be gone, and all the wild things will be dead or in zoos."

He swung back to his desk and picked up a pencil, turning it slowly with one hand. "I used to think we could stop it. I used to think people would demand that we stop short of taming every inch of the planet. But in the last few years I've wised up."

Grabbing the pencil with both hands, he tested its strength by bending it against his thumbs. "Most people don't need wild places or wild things. They like the *idea* of an arctic refuge and the *idea* of free-roaming caribou. But given the choice between those things and saving a nickel a gallon, the pocketbooks and the gas guzzlers always win."

At that moment the pencil added the appropriate punctuation by snapping in two. For an instant Kirby Rogers lost his cool long enough to show a flash of embarrassment but quickly recovered, casually toss-ing the two halves into his wastebasket. "Your friend Roland Taft needed wild places and wild things."

"Yeah, he did. And that's why I'm here." Kirby had given me a smooth handoff, but I still fumbled the play, not eager to introduce the formality of my questions into the curious intimacy that had devel-oped between us. In the end I had no choice but to break the mood. "You see, I had some questions about what happened down there. I'm especially disturbed by the gun your guys found."

Kirby Rogers gave me a blank look. "The gun? What about it?"

I played for time by clearing my throat. "Well, you see, Roland never carried a gun in bear country. The reason I know that is because he told me. And he even put it in writing."

His eyes sharpened and his voice roughened. "Are you talking about his diatribe in *New Age Naturalist?* Where he called me a liar?"

Before I figured out how to smooth that over, Kirby Rogers plunged on, this time with words designed to raise my hackles. "You know what your problem is, Mrs. Maxwell? The guy had you snowed. Completely. You really went for the Saint Roland of the Bears act, didn't you?"

I hate instant psychoanalysis from complete strangers. I hate being called Mrs. Maxwell. I hate having anyone think I've been duped. But most of all, I hate opening my mouth just in time to stick my foot in. So I just sat there, saying nothing. Not that I needed to. Oh, no. Kirby Rogers was on a tear, ready to do the talking for both of us.

"That seems to be the prevailing view among airheads. That Roland Taft was some kind of romantic and pacifist saint." He lowered his fisted hands to the desktop. "I do not share that opinion. To me, Roland Taft was a seriously disturbed misanthrope with a crafty way of torpedoing the work and reputation of his competitors."

Finally I found my voice. "What kind of man he was is not the issue. How he died is." I gave myself a count of three. "Have you traced the gun your people found down there?"

For another second or so Kirby Rogers glared at me

across two feet of desktop and then he sighed. "We tried and came up empty, but so what? There are literally millions of guns floating around out there. Why should anyone be surprised that a kook like Roland Taft lied about owning one?"

I let the pejorative pass without comment. "What about his cabin? Have you searched it?"

"Searched it? We haven't even found it." He spread his hands. "Excuse me for asking, but why bother?"

That got to me. That any scientist, even one of the bureaucratic variety, could overlook the importance of preserving a dead colleague's research, the notes and papers that are the lifeblood of science. When I said as much, Kirby Rogers suddenly looked like a man trying to swallow a grin.

He picked up his phone and punched a button. "Julianne? Bring me the grant proposal that came in from Roland Taft."

In the time it took his assistant to locate the file, Kirby Rogers and I did our best to avoid eye contact. The surface intimacy was gone, blasted to bits by his disdain for Roland and my determination not to underrate my friend. When his assistant came through the door, he gave us a quick introduction. "Lauren Maxwell. Julianne Blanchard."

I got to my feet and took the hand she offered. Her shake was limp and her eyes owlish behind large wire-rims. I'd thought Vanessa described her as mousy because of her dust-colored hair but decided now that there was more to the description than just one detail. Everything about Julianne Blanchard seemed tentative and timid. She even scurried like a mouse when she left the office, needing only a *squeak-squeak-squeak* to complete the portrait.

Kirby Rogers had dismissed his assistant from his mind even before she left his office, pausing only long enough for that cursory introduction before continuing our conversation. "A quick review of Taft's publications shows his best work was long behind him. Lately he'd focused on questionable journals like *New Age Naturalist.*" His smile took on a nasty twist. "And his concerns tended to be eccentric, if not bizarre."

The door shut quietly behind Julianne Blanchard just as her boss leaned across the desk to hand me a sheaf of papers from the file she'd delivered. One of the tricks of our business is the ability to quickly scan paperwork, deduce the relevant conclusions, and be prepared to argue intelligently in a matter of seconds, but Roland's grant proposal stopped me cold right at the top of page one, in the spot earmarked for a statement of intent. Roland needed only one of the lines left blank to explain his purpose: "To prove that *Ursus arctos horribilis* are deities."

After staring at that line for several minutes, I finally raised my eyes and met the amusement in those of Kirby Rogers. "Your friend wasn't kidding, Mrs. Maxwell. He thought of himself as Saint Roland. And he thought that grizzly bears were gods."

10

Denial is the first stage of grief. My immediate impulse upon learning that my friend literally worshiped grizzlies was to dismiss both the idea and the man who voiced it. Kirby Rogers just sat there with a smirk marring the handsome symmetry of his face. I, on the other hand, shot to my feet and, trembling with indignation, came up with a line straight out of a 1950s B-movie. "I don't have to listen to garbage like that from somebody like you." Then I spun on my heel and stormed out of his office, ignoring his assistant, who finally squeaked like a good little mouse as I marched past.

My knees started quaking and my stomach started quivering before I got to the street. So much for the *film noir* exit. In Hollywood the director yells "Cut!" before his leading lady falls apart, but this wasn't simply a bad movie. Or even a bad dream. Losing a good friend was hard enough. Learning that the friend wigged out before he died promised a double-whammy of mourning—for the man and for his mind. Too much! I rejected the idea out of hand. And yet . . .

"To prove that *Ursus arctos horribilis* are deities." Roland's statement of intent was preserved in my mind's eye with the awful clarity of a photograph. I stumbled to the 4-Runner, trying to blank the page of memory. And yet . . .

"To prove that *Ursus arctos horribilis* are deities." His voice intoned the words that echoed in my ears. I jammed a cassette into the player, desperate to erase the tape of memory. And yet . . .

"To prove that *Ursus arctos horribilis* are deities." The page remained indelibly etched and the tape forever looped in my mind. Saying it ain't so don't necessarily mean it ain't. The number one rule of science says that when the data doesn't verify the premise, it's time to get a new hypothesis. My theory that Roland Taft never carried a firearm in bear country was not borne out by the on-scene data, including that damned gun which couldn't be traced. The time had come to consider the possibility that the man who died at McNeil River was no longer the man I remembered.

Working out of my home has plenty of drawbacks, but for jobs like this being surrounded by the creature comforts helps plenty. To settle my stomach and weak knees, I brewed up some tea in the quiet kitchen while I got organized. With Nina at the clinic, Jake looking for an errant airplane with Travis MacDonald, and Jessie carpooled to dance class, I had a good two hours before my home erupted with end-of-the-day pandemonium.

Coming up with a new hypothesis requires reviewing what is known and sifting for what might have been overlooked. For the most part, my reviewing and sifting could be done by telephone, a simple canvass of the leading bear scientists and journals to confirm that Roland had, in fact, lost his mind. I carried a pot of Red Rose to my office at the back of the house and started to work the phone.

The grand old man of bear biologists lived in Montana, hard by Yellowstone National Park, whose rangers stopped asking for advice when it became apparent that he cared more for grizzlies than for tourists. Of Roland Taft, he knew little. "Never lived up to his early promise, did he?" The opinion was delivered in a quavering tone, which owed as much to satellite telephone links as to age. "Too undisciplined, I suspect. Had some interesting ideas about learned behavior, but we hadn't seen much from him in the last year or two."

The Young Turk in bear biology was a Canadian who did his research in the Rockies around Banff and his teaching in the flatlands around Edmonton. But the lilt in his voice was pure Québecois. "Roland Taft? For him I think the focus was learned behavior." A long drawn out *aaahhhhh* and then an apology. "I mean no disrespect, but may I say that science did not come first with Roland? No, for him comes first the bears and the wilderness. And living free among the wild things."

The current editor of the professional journal of bear biologists sounded relieved when I promised to do my best to locate Roland's current research. "I need his paper on learned behavior for my last issue, which comes out early next year." The panic subsided, but the whine remained in her tone. "You have no idea what a burden this editorship has been. I can't tell you how many deadlines have been missed with no apologies. Roland Taft was one of the worst offenders. With him it was always a little more time, a little more research. Three years we've been waiting."

A scientist can generate a lot of paper in three years, and I wanted to see Roland's. Kirby Rogers might have dismissed my friend as a kook, but apparently nobody else in the world of bear biology had. Three years of field data fills a lot of notebooks. I visualized neat stacks of rubber-banded index cards on a rude desk and a shelf full of spiral notebooks hanging above. If Roland's cabin could be found, Belle Doyon would find it. Before tracking her down, I decided to try Cal Williamson once again. After all, the pilot who ferried me to and from McNeil River was probably the last person to see and talk to Roland Taft. If he happened to know the location of Roland's camp, he might be able to save me a lot of time and trouble. If he knew *and* happened to feel like sharing that knowledge. We certainly hadn't parted on friendly terms.

Turned out that neither absence nor distance had softened Cal Williamson's heart toward me. Our telephone conversation was very brief and barely civil. Had he delivered supplies to Roland Taft? "Once or twice." Did he know the location of Roland's camp? "Nope." Did he drop supplies? "Nope." Did Roland meet him somewhere? "Yup." Where? "On the beach." At McNeil Cove? "Nope." Where? "North a ways, past the Paint River." Would he show me the place? "Nope." Could I hire him to show me? "Nope." Next week? "Never."

At that point I swallowed a scream, took a deep

breath, and then tried again. "Look, Mr. Williamson, since you don't even know me, I can't even begin to imagine what you've got against me. But, obviously, you've got a problem."

Silence on the other end of the phone. I took another deep breath. "I've got a problem, too. One of my best friends is dead. I'd like to know how it happened. And why it happened. And I don't even know why he wanted to see me."

More silence. Another deep breath. "I know he used your radio to call me. The connection was bad, but I thought he said something about bears being missing?"

Another deep breath but from his end this time. "Yup."

I tried to keep the eagerness out of my voice. "He said bears were missing?"

"Yup."

Believe it or not, it's possible to detect signs of irritation in monosyllabic replies, especially those that come back to back. Still, I persisted. Here was my chance to clear up one of the growing number of mysteries surrounding Roland Taft's death. "Do you know what he meant?"

"Nope." A sharp intake of breath. "And that's all the questions I got time for today."

Cal Williamson hung up with such force that my left ear rang for half an hour. The nuisance of that proved no distraction as I concentrated on examining the facets of the problem—the unexpected gun, the missing bears, the improbable assertion of grizzly divinity, and the feud between Kirby Rogers and Roland Taft. No matter which facet I held up to the light, the reflection contained the image of one man.

Who said the gun couldn't be traced? Kirby Rogers. Who said Roland Taft believed bears were gods? Kirby Rogers. Who was the target of Roland's scientific wrath? Kirby Rogers. Who stood to lose if McNeil River bears were missing? Kirby Rogers. Now more than ever, I needed to find Roland Taft's cabin. To do that, I first had to find my Athabascan friend, Belle Doyon.

Belle reveres the old ways and has devoted herself to mastering the ancient skills that enabled her people to flourish in a punishing climate. She can weave a reed basket, run a dog team, trap a wolf, tan a hide, net a chinook, and build an igloo. Her life is dictated by the seasons. In winter she runs a trapline to snare beaver, wolf, and lynx. Spring before breakup is spent on smaller game—rabbit, grouse, muskrat, and duck. May clears the last ice from the river and sandhill cranes fly overhead, signaling the imminent return of the fish. July brings king salmon up the river, and in August come the silver and dog salmon. By October the Yukon runs with ice again, and Belle concentrates on getting in her moose and her firewood before the river locks down for winter.

The calendar hanging above my desk counted down the days until June, meaning Belle could be anywhere. In another three weeks I would make book on finding her in a summer encampment along the Yukon, spending the long, warm days repairing her gear and picking berries while a fish wheel plucked salmon from the river. A month ago she would certainly have been found at her cabin outside Tanana, tanning the last of her hides with the help of the grandmother who raised her. Where she might be today was anybody's guess.

I patched a call through to the post office in Tanana, only to discover that Belle was in Anchorage, tending to her grandmother, who'd been admitted to the native hospital with an unspecified complaint. A few minutes later I had a kind-hearted nurse on the phone who assured me that Mrs. Doyon was doing great and promised that the next voice I heard would be Belle's. She wasn't kidding.

"Hello? Lauren? Is that you?"

Even the most obstinate unreconstructed native can handle a telephone these days, but Belle's voice still rang with discomfort. For a woman who thinks nothing of trusting a decrepit flying machine to set her down safely in places devoid of landing strips, she can be awfully suspicious of technology. She once told me that the disembodied voice coming over the phone reminds her of the talking spirits in Athabascan myth, and she insists that a person of wisdom must see a man's eyes to gauge the truth of his words.

"It's me, all right. How's your granny?"

"Very old and very stubborn." She laughed gently. "But no longer very blind. The doctors fixed her eyes good. This season she'll find the choicest berry by sight instead of touch." The humor disappeared from her voice. "And you? You wintered good?"

After bringing her quickly up to date on my family, I told Belle about Roland Taft's death and my desire to find his cabin. She listened quietly, evincing neither surprise at the circumstances of his death nor curiosity about my reason for wanting to find his camp. At her suggestion we agreed to begin our search in another two days, which left her time to make arrangements for other family members to keep her grandmother company. In the meantime, she wanted every bit of information I had about the possible location. I suggested we talk over dinner, but Belle wanted to stay with Granny until she fell asleep.

"I will leave here at sunset. About eleven o'clock. Is that too late for me to visit?"

"Not at all. My monsters will be asleep, meaning you'll be spared getting tackled when they answer the door and find you on the step."

Also meaning I'd be spared the embarrassment of serving a native guest some of my family's low-fat, high-veggie lean cuisine. A couple of thousand years of necessity has left Alaska's natives with physical and cultural cravings for animal fats, liquid if possible. Their notion of fresh food is moose with the hide on, still warm and still bloody. Outside of berries and roots, the only vegetable traditionally consumed is willow buds. Being overrun by the white man hasn't improved native nutrition much. Alcohol's the big hit, of course. Beyond the booze, there's tea and pilot bread and potato chips. In other words, caffeine, starch, and junk food. So much for the benefits of exposing a "primitive" culture to the "achievements" of Western civilization.

I spent the hours before Belle's arrival trying to narrow the field of our search. I knew Roland had wintered over in King Salmon once or twice, working menial jobs to get together a grubstake for the next summer's research. Cal Williamson said they'd met on the beach near the Paint River, north of the sanctuary at McNeil Cove. Maybe Roland had decided to go farther afield for his research. Ten months of the year brown bears were hard to find at the McNeil River. And in the two months of the year that the grizzlies were in residence, the only rival to their population was the throng of bear biologists who descended on the falls each summer. Research-wise, McNeil River had been done. Maybe those missed deadlines of Roland's represented his decision to open up his inquiry in a whole new place.

Belle Doyon had come to the same conclusion by the time she arrived. I asked if she knew the area.

"I've flown it, but I've never been on the ground there." She tossed her head, flinging her black braids over her shoulders. "Nothing there but tundra. And the wind. Not a place the Déné ever lived. Nobody else, too."

Facing an arctic wind that gathered in Siberia before picking up speed and power over the storm-tossed Bering Sea, who'd even bother trying? Certainly not Roland Taft. He knew enough to look for a snug forest clearing that offered protection from the wind and plenty of fuel for his fire. We agreed to try our luck farther inland where fingers of boreal spruce forest reached into the Alaska peninsula. I told her that Cal Williamson refused to fly us and that suddenly all the other pilots in the area were all booked up, too. She just shrugged. "John will give us a plane. You pilot yet?"

"Me?" I took a step back. "Not yet. Not ever!"

Belle shrugged again and shook her head. "Then maybe we have to wait to come out until John's pilots fly back. We take food for one week."

That was longer than I wanted to be away from home, but I'd learned not to argue with Belle Doyon. A wise Athabascan plans for the worst. In the 125 generations that Alaska has been their home, experience has taught Athabascans that the worst is what usually comes.

11

For two days we trudged down game trails walled by a thick poplar scrub that clutched at our shoulders and provided safe haven to all manner of predators, including some that considered us likely prey. The small brass bell from a Tibetan temple that I'd hung from my backpack tinkled at every step, offering a muddled combination of instant karma to me and early warning to lurking beasts. And no doubt annoying Belle Doyon almost as much as it reassured me. Whenever she stopped to listen or look or sniff the air, I jammed my fingers inside the bell to secure the tiny clapper. Minimizing potential distractions seemed the least I could do to help her locate Roland's cabin and safeguard us on the trail. Keeping my mouth shut except in camp was another component of that strategy.

And the most difficult component, as it turned out, because Alaska's bush always makes me feel like singing, even in winter. In summer, forget it. The month of May starts with sixteen hours of sunlight. Add to that a daily gain of five minutes of light, and you've got plenty of sunshine to transform bare winter branches into lush summer foliage with hardly a stop for spring.

Something similar happens inside me each year when I roll up my winter sleeves and find the first promise of summer in the lengthening days. The caress of warm air sprouts a tendril of hope in my soul, and the dazzle of brilliant light inspires a song of joy in my heart. Rebirth or resurrection, call it what you will. There is something of heaven in those long, lovely days. Heaven enough to make me forget the mournful purpose of our search. Heaven enough to divert me from the uncomfortable irony of finding myself simultaneously attracted to and suspicious of Kirby Rogers. Heaven enough to help me overcome the claustrophobia engendered by the endless maze of green tunnels through which we walked.

Just after noon on the third day, we broke free of the poplars and found Roland's cabin. Maybe Belle sensed the human presence snugged into a small clearing amidst all that wildness. Maybe unintentional clues left by the man himself led her to his home—a strand of golden hair, thread of man-made fleece strung from a poplar twig. Or maybe the land itself guided her steps, offering first the soggy muskeg and barren tundra as guideposts of places not fit for human habitation and then the gurgling dips and tucks of a creek drainage crested by a raw-boned ridge that soared above forested slopes. Belle didn't say and I didn't ask, but only followed her across the swift creek and out of the thick greenery to emerge into a narrow meadow that sloped gently uphill to a tidy cabin tucked under the spreading branches of an ancient spruce.

"Your friend lived here, I think." Belle swung the pack off her back and leaned it against an old stump crowned with an enamel tabletop which showed a fair bit of rust. "All around here is bear sign."

My eyes were drawn to the spruce, to the ropes swinging in neat ranks from a stout branch, ropes which Roland relied on to survive among the grizzly. I slipped the pack from my back and lowered it gently to the grass before crossing the meadow to knot my fingers over the thick strands of rope. The daily practice of his hands had smoothed the roughness from the hemp. But there had been no tree for Roland to climb on the Mikfik sedge flats. He found there only a few moments of unutterable terror followed by an instant of agony and everlasting death. With conscious effort I freed myself from Roland's ropes and turned back toward my living friend. "This is the place, Belle. Thanks for finding it."

She ducked her head, averting her eyes as she wandered back toward the stream. I took a deep breath and let it out slowly. Modern mothers-to-be learn the cleansing breath in birthing class, and most soon discover that the usefulness of the technique extends far beyond the stress of the delivery room. Sufficiently armored once again, I lifted the latch on Roland Taft's door.

Except for a few stray beams of light seeping into the cabin from two shuttered windows and the brilliant square in the shape of the opened door, gloom festooned the interior. Even so, the tumult shone through, visible in the scatter of cans framed by the door light and discernable in the vague tumble of somethings beyond. I picked my way through the room to throw back the shutters on both windows before really surveying the devastation.

Trashed. That's the best description I can give of what had been done to the cabin. Every drawer of the desk had been wrenched out and flung to the floor. Above, the shelf I'd imagined filled with notebooks hung at a crazy angle, empty even of dust. As my eyes registered the computer tossed in a corner, my mind registered the inevitable question—power source?—before both swept on. To a season's stock of canned food strewn from pantry cupboard clear across the floor to the narrow cot spread with a jumbled quilt. To the camera mixed among a collapsed bundle of kindling beside the wood stove. To the flung binoculars, which lay amidst a toss of pens and pencils, including a rainbow of subtle shades destined to illustrate his research. To the shortwave radio upended in the corner on a pile of well-thumbed magazines. To the unbroken mirror hanging beside the bed, a mirror which reflected my face in a curious quartet—the Lauren Maxwell of today surrounded by photographs of the girl I left behind.

My heart somersaulted then. Not for what I was or who I'd been, but for what I'd never understood. All those years I'd called Roland Taft my friend, he'd wanted to be something more. That's why he'd saved the blurry snapshot from a finals rush at SUNY Buffalo. That's why he'd torn my half of the portrait from one of the first Christmas cards Max and I had sent as a couple. And that's why he'd clipped out the photograph the newspapers used when my husband disappeared. Determined student, happy wife, and haggard widow—the friendship we shared had embraced each of those phases of my life and left me a debt outstanding. The least I owed my friend was figuring out why he died.

That there was a why beyond bad luck or statistical inevitability was evidenced by the havoc within Roland's cabin. A thieving animal would have passed up the canned goods, preferring the sacks of flour, sugar, beans, and rice undisturbed beneath the pantry cupboard. Generally, Alaska's bush features two subspecies of thieving humans—hungry and larcenous. The hungry variety goes straight for the food, and the larcenous variety goes straight for the goods. The human who'd so thoroughly tossed Roland Taft's cabin had left both the stock of food and the array of electronics. Meaning he'd been looking for something else. But what?

After spending a few minutes wading through the mess, I had my answer. I started with the debris from the desk, pawing through the papers in search of the notebooks and field journals kept by every fame-seeking scientist since Henry Oldenburg invented scientific journalism with the publication in 1665 of his *Philosophical Transactions*. Nothing.

I lifted the shortwave radio off the pile of magazines and shook them one by one, hoping to shake free a scrap from Roland's work-in-progress. Nothing.

I backtracked down the trail of wires leading from the abandoned computer to his work station, searching for the floppy disks that fit into the twin drives of his PC. Nothing.

No notebooks, no rough drafts, no computer disks. The only things inside that cabin that even hinted at Roland's scientific occupation were an artist's pad containing sketches of bears and a tattered corner ripped from what looked to have been a chart of bear migrations. Whoever had trashed Roland Taft's cabin had carefully sifted for his science and removed everything except the torn shred of chart tacked up beside his work station.

I was reluctant to take the next logical step until Belle's appearance in the doorway forced me to face the facts. Our eyes met across the mess. "It's gone, Belle. There's nothing here at all."

Her glance swept the cluttered interior of Roland's cabin, leaving me to trip over my tongue like the greenest *cheechako* confronted for the first time with the essential simplicity of Déné ways. "His work, I mean. That's what gone. But he left everything else." I waved my hands around rather vaguely. "As you can see."

Her visual examination continued, pausing now to focus on particulars—a corner, a chair, a shelf. She stepped forward and then stopped, hovering just inside the door. The Déné have strong taboos about death. The name of a dead relative is never mentioned, and the possessions of the dead must be abandoned or destroyed. Finally Belle overcame her hesitation and continued across the room to a darkly shadowed corner. Reaching out, she plucked from the shadows a rifle I hadn't noticed. She held it out to me. "He left this, too, your friend? His weapon?"

I started to answer, but Belle was concentrating on the rifle. With the sure grip of an expert, she turned it in her hands, looking it over carefully. Then she opened the action and checked the magazine. Empty.

Three swift steps brought her to the shelf which had earlier drawn her eyes. Now her hand followed and came up with a cartridge box. She flicked the box toward me but it fluttered to the floor. Empty. "His weapon he leaves. His ammunition he takes?"

"I don't think so." I picked up the empty cartridge box and tucked it into a pocket. "Roland never carried a weapon in grizzly country. He said bears feared the gun more than man." I shrugged and turned away. "I don't think my friend took anything. I think another man left this mess. After he took what he came for."

"Your friend had wisdom. The one who came after flew in." She spoke quietly, merely reciting the facts. "One man and maybe more."

I spun back to face her. "What do you mean?"

"I found his sign in another clearing." Her braids danced when she tossed her head toward the north. "Helicopter tracks. And, nearby, two bears. Dead." She answered my question before I could ask it. "Both killed by the same man. Maybe from helicopter. Maybe not."

The facts boiled inside me, bubbling up like an evil stew that threatened to sicken my soul as well as my heart. The man who tossed Roland's cabin had several areas of expertise. For instance, flying a helicopter. And hunting down bears. Not to mention the discriminating eye of a scientist.

Boiling, seething—those facts burned within me, a poisonous threat until Belle released me with her touch. The fingers that closed around my arm brought me back. "I must tend to the bears."

Reading my confusion from my face, Belle explained. "Before time began, all were equals—animals and man. Man killed and ate animals. Animals killed and ate man. Then came Tsa-o-sha, the powerful one who brought many gifts to the Déné. He killed the bad animals and made them good like they are today. But he never killed bear."

I nodded. Taboo and ritual and ceremonialism still had a place in her life, offering guideposts for correct behavior and the proper order of things. What I wouldn't have given right then for my own share of simplicity. "What will you do, Belle?"

She pulled the tanned hide bag from her belt and dug out a knife. Once every Athabascan carried both a workbag on the waist and a fire bag around the neck. A man's workbag included a knife, awl, drill, and lancet. A woman's workbag contained a snowshoe needle, awl, drill, knife, skin scraper, and sinew thread. In the fire bag both sexes carried the same rig: a bit of *Fomes igniarius* (also known as false tinder fungus), wood shavings, and a cord for sparking off the drill. Belle tested the edge of her knife and drew a drop of blood. "Take his skull and put it at the top of a spruce. The eyes must look north."

I tried to hide the shudder that rattled through me at the thought of such bloody work. I tried even harder to inject some enthusiasm into the offer I felt obligated to make. "Need some help?"

For the first time all day a tiny smile tugged at her lips. Her eyes swept the cabin once more. "No. Your place is here."

With that, Belle turned and left Roland Taft's home, seeming almost eager to escape and honor her demons. Leaving me alone to wrestle with mine.

12

While Belle Doyon practiced the ritual of her people, I devoted my time to a traditional way a white woman handles stress. I cleaned house. Not out of guilt for failing to understand the depth of Roland's feelings for me. And not to escape the ferment of suspicions still boiling inside. The practicalities of the Alaskan bush dictated my decision to set Roland's cabin to rights. The day would certainly come when some fortunate soul would be very grateful to stumble upon the food and shelter it offered.

The first job was finding Roland's elevated cache so I had a place to put the canned and bulk foods from the cabin. Otherwise, as time passed, critters small and large would find their way into the cabin and eat everything up. Eventually the little guys would get to the beans, rice, flour, and sugar anyway. Nothing but a locked vault can keep mice, rats, lemmings, squirrels, and pikas out for long. But the tinned food could be secured against bears by getting the cans high enough off the ground to be out of reach of nonclimbing grizzlies. Left in the cabins, the cans would soon be squashed flat by marauding bears who would lap up the contents left dripping from walls and floors.

In searching for the cache, I wound up answering the question of how Roland powered his computer. No great investigative triumph there. I simply followed the power line tacked up from a corner of the cabin to the creek and found a Pelton wheel submerged in the fast-running water. How like Roland to have gone to all the trouble of hauling a generator to this remote spot but not bothering to bring along other "necessities" to sop up the surplus power. No TV, electric lights, VCRs, or clock radios for my pal. The PC was a must, but, for the rest, he relied on sourdough ways.

The cache turned up nearby, a sturdy box of two-by-eights atop a platform created by nailing crossbeams between three living alders a height of fifteen feet. Roland's homemade ladder lay on the ground below, twined by shoots from a tangle of new growth. After yanking the ladder free, I propped it against the platform, opened the cache, and started to work.

Stack and carry, stack and carry, stack and carry. Piling up cans and then lugging them by the boxload across stony ground is the kind of monotonous work that frees the mind for wandering. Mine wanted to follow Belle Doyon and ogle her bloody handiwork, but I refused to allow that. Instead, I gave in and faced the fountain of facts threatening to ulcerate my insides. What my friend Vanessa said about Kirby Rogers was true. With his fine looks, he was any woman's beefcake. Witness my own reaction to those gorgeous brown eyes. What she hadn't said—and probably didn't know—was that his beauty was definitely no more than skin deep. Judging by what I'd heard in his office and seen in Roland's cabin, that fine exterior which Kirby Rogers flaunted served to camouflage a decidedly more common interior: *Scumbag americanus.*

I juggled the final load of Beanie Weenies up the ladder and heaved them inside the cache. Kirby Rogers was the answer to every *Who?* that I came up with. Who could fly a helicopter, slay the wily grizzly, and cull every scientifically significant paper from the cabin? Who said the gun found with Roland's body couldn't be traced? Who said my friend worshiped grizzlies? Who was the target of Roland's scorn? Who stood to lose if there were problems with the bears at the McNeil River sanctuary? Kirby Rogers, Kirby Rogers, Kirby Rogers, Kirby Rogers. I had only one other question. Was Roland's death simply a bit of fortuitous luck that eliminated Kirby's problem or something more sinister? That question I couldn't answer. Yet.

After returning to the cabin, I decided against trying to lug the sacks of staples without Belle's help and started tidying the interior. The computer looked okay, but something inside rattled ominously. The camera, binoculars, and shortwave radio had ridden out the storm undamaged and wound up on the desk. One, two, three—the desk drawers slid in. Four, five, six—a short stack of papers filled each. Straightening the shelf above required driving in a new nail. When that was done, only odds and ends remained.

I gathered up the pens and pencils and sat down on Roland's cot to look through his sketchpad. His drawings of bears showed the full range of color in the species: silver tip, blond, yellow, and every shade of brown. Every animal had a name, and he'd captured the individual characteristics of each depicted—the massive forepaws of a mature boar named Zeus, the coiled readiness of a nursing sow called Amelia, and the playfulness and timidity of twin cubs named for superstar biologists, Linne and Darwin. I fanned through the pages, reading the names and dates and locations, wondering which of the bears so lovingly recorded had been the one to end Roland's life.

Nothing in the sketchbook even hinted at the direction of Roland's current research. For that, I turned to the shred of chart tacked up by his workstation, a simple enough configuration with individual animals listed vertically and what appeared to be a horizontal index of life-cycle behaviors—denning, emergence, estrus. From what little was left, I guessed that Roland had been tracking individual bears for several years. Lots of individual bears. Suddenly his message about "missing" bears made a little more sense. After all, he wasn't studying bears in general but specific animals, individual bears he recognized. Individual bears who were missing?

Just then Belle returned from her grisly chore, dripping creek water from her arms and knife blade. Together we lugged the last of the food up to Roland's cache and secured the hasp with a stout stick. Belle started a small fire outside the cabin and boiled water for tea while I shuttered Roland's home for the last time. We ate pilot bread and cheese with our tea, and while we ate, Belle told me about the dead bears.

"That work is really for a man. Woman should avoid the bear." She wrapped both hands around her cup of tea and grinned at me from across the fire. "No problem today. Both were females."

"Young females?" Belle's joke fell flat because my immediate reaction was concern for the population consequences of losing two females. "Not breeding, I hope."

"One maybe." She shrugged. "The other was very old. In her last season, probably."

I nodded, sipped some of the hot tea from my battered Sierra cup, and then tried to pick up the joke I'd let drop. "So female bears don't mind human females?"

"Bears like females best of all. That's why no man sleeps with his woman before hunting. No hunter wants a woman smell on him."

So much for feminism among the Déné. And while bear scientists and park rangers still debate whether it's safe to have sex in bear country or travel through while menstruating, the natives who live with the grizzly speak with one voice: NO! Belle explained that women never eat the flesh of a bear, and a pregnant woman also avoids seeing bears or sleeping on their skins. Stepping on bear bones brings bad luck to anybody, so Belle had been careful to move the carcasses off the game trail. The Déné view life as a circle and leaving bones on a path prevents an animal's return to life. For the same reason the bones of a fish and feathers of a goose are thrown into the river. Once reborn, the Déné figure the fish and geese will return to their old haunts and provide supper all over again. While dead, some animals have powerful spirits, especially the bear.

"The bear killer marks each of his children with charcoal to protect them." Belle set her cup down and demonstrated, rubbing cinders onto her forehead. "Then he hangs the skin on his door to show his worth."

"How was a bear killed before rifles arrived?" Some natives wouldn't know but not Belle. The white man's gift of liquor had killed both of her parents and deeply scarred her childhood. She'd spent much of her life since learning the traditions of her people and sometimes rediscovering those ways. "I can't believe any bow could throw an arrow hard enough to kill a grizzly."

"What you say is true. Not bow and arrow for bears. A spear. But first you find the bear." She got to her feet to demonstrate again and pranced around the fire. "Find and then track. And singing bear songs. Some songs make the bear happy. Some songs make the bear angry."

"Which kind does the hunter sing?"

"Songs to make the bear angry. So he will charge." She stopped suddenly and knelt on one knee, clenched hands upraised to hold an imaginary spear. "Never rest the spear on the ground, or the bear will drive it into the earth. Lift and he goes up on his legs, swinging his feet, cutting his feet, presenting his heart to the hunter." She sprang up, stabbing the empty air. "And then the bear is dead. Or the man is dead."

I shuddered, knowing which it would be in my case. "I would be scared stiff. Literally."

Belle dropped her arms and turned to face me. "Great fear brings great courage. That is why we honor the bear and also his killer."

Less than an hour later we were back on the trail, quickly putting distance between us and Roland's cabin. With all of his papers gone, there was no reason for me to stay, and Belle had reasons of her own for wanting to leave. There is no time for loafing in the life of the Déné, especially in a place of the dead. Every day in the life of Belle's people was a fight for survival, with each season bringing a new challenge. In the long, lovely days of summer, a woman like Belle needed to be in camp beside a river, gutting and drying a winter's supply of fish scooped from the water by a fish wheel. Plus her old granny waited at the native hospital in Anchorage.

As a rule, I find coming back harder than going out, probably because of my reluctance to leave the bush for the mundane workaday world of the city. This was the exception to the rule. The disgust nipping at my heels made my steps more eager, disgust with myself for finding Kirby Rogers attractive and disgust with him for turning out to be pretty ordinary after all.

We walked through the evening and into the night, knowing the difference only by the increasing slant of the golden sunlight. Belle led without pausing to look or listen or sniff the air, guided by her memories of the trip in. Sometime after nine a breeze sprang up that carried with it the salty tang of the sea. Our path led us into the wind and that's what got us into trouble. The breeze carried the human scent and bell sound away from the grazing bears.

A sow with twin cubs, and we got ourselves between Mama and her babies before either of us realized she was there. I heard the sow before I spotted her, a hoarse *whoof-whoof-whoof* that stiffened the hair on my neck and arms.

Belle stopped in midstride. "Lauren, back up slowly."

I'd taken just three glacial steps when the cubs

chimed in with a chorus of whining bleats. Keeping my voice to a whisper instead of a scream hurt like hell. "Jesus, Belle, they're behind me."

Up ahead, the sow was on her hind legs, head waving back and forth, still whoofing. Belle started to ease the workbag off her belt and broke into a wordless song, almost a chant, interspersed with a series of terse directions. She was careful to speak my name before giving me guidance. "Lauren, do not look in her eyes."

For a moment I was happy to focus on those enormous feet. And then I saw the three-inch claws. A step ahead, Belle shivered. My panic was infectious.

"Lauren, do not run."

That's just what I wanted to do. I wanted to turn and run for the nearest tree. Except there were no trees at hand. Just as there had been no trees for Roland. A scream bubbled in my throat.

"Lauren, do not yell."

Step by step, we backed away from the sow. Each step brought us closer to her cubs. On hind legs the bear looked huge. She dropped down to all fours and looked even scarier.

"Lauren, I will drop my bag to give her our scent."

Suddenly the cubs squealed. Belle tossed her workbag a dozen feet up the path. And the grizzly sow charged.

She reached the bag in an instant, her feet a mere blur of motion. Back we scurried, a little faster, finally even with the cubs.

"Lauren, if she charges again, stand still. She may stop."

The sow had the bag in her mouth, gnashing it with sharp teeth and growling. Step back, step back, step back, now past the cubs, who scuttled toward Mama, bleating. The sow stiffened and dropped the workbag as her cubs ran past.

"Lauren, if she doesn't stop, drop down and play dead. The pack may protect you."

Mother, may I? The sow whoofed and then whoofed again. When Belle stopped, so did I, braced for the attack and ready to drop. Fetal position. On your side. Hands behind neck. What good would it do? Didn't you see those teeth? Can't you see those claws?

Another whoof and the sow turned away, following her cubs back up the trail. And then I heard a child sobbing. When Belle reached out to squeeze my shoulder, I realized the cries came from me.

13

The grizzly sow robbed me of my self-respect. Part of it, anyway. The big-screen entertainment of movies and small-screen infotainment of television stimulate our imaginations to fantasize how we'd react to confronting a monster. In the secure little world of my mind's eye, I always came through my crucible of terror with dignity intact. In our secret hearts, don't we all? If nature threw me a horror like a great white shark, I imagined besting the fish with superior intelligence. If society threw me a bogeyman like a slavering serial killer, I imagined defeating the creep with transcendent courage. When, in fact, fate threw me a real live Alaskan brown bear, I cried. There's Belle Doyon, the very essence of stoicism, cool and authoritative in facing the beast. Here's Lauren Maxwell, patched together from baser materials, a sniveling and quivering tub of cowardice. Crying! No one ever imagines crying. No one. Not ever. Especially when one masquerades as a modern, enlightened woman of the postindustrial era who is looking forward to the challenges of the twenty-first century, thank you very much.

In another way, that growling old girl did me a helluva favor. Even as her appearance on the trail infused me with limb-deadening and brain-numbing fear, her awesome reality kindled a beacon fire that succeeded in delivering me back to *my* Roland Taft. The process begun by phone calls to the world's foremost bear authorities and accelerated by the visit to Roland's cabin was irrevocably completed by the face-to-face with the grizzly sow. Gone forever was Kirby Rogers's looney-tunes version of my friend. Back for good—and admitted with pride—was Saint Roland of the Bears. After that encounter, I felt fresh respect for both the grizzly and the friend who dedicated his life to their survival. Roland's ability to live among the bears proved he was neither a back-stabbing coward nor a delusional kook. Maybe I couldn't explain the grizzly-as-deity grant proposal, but who cared? What mattered now was finding out why a man who for years safely shared his territory with dozens of bears wound up getting killed by one. Statistical inevitability and bad luck might be the twin poles of official thinking, but neither cut it with me anymore. No more bureaucratic BS. I wanted the truth and intended to get it.

Before I could follow through on that intention, I had to get in some family time. Working parents lead a schizo existence, constantly juggling the competing needs of work and home. These days Jake's nonschool hours were mostly spent helping Travis MacDonald search for a rogue pilot who'd had two near-misses in the crowded skies above Anchorage. That plus the afterglow from our expedition to return the wolf pup meant my boy's immediate needs were met. Jessie, however, hadn't had a good dose of mother love since the afternoon I'd spent visiting her classroom. The present focus of her life was dance school's end-of-the-year recital. I'd missed the first two performances of *Tales and Legends* while bushwhacking with Belle Doyon. Normally I'd have postponed life itself before missing that kind of red-letter kid activity, but Roland Taft's death had left things decidedly unnormal. Fortunately, Nina and Jake had been on hand the first night to watch my little girl leap and pirouette to Disney's version of *Alice in Wonderland*. My last chance to see Jess strut her stuff in a two-tone pink tutu came just six hours after I arrived home. Spending an evening with the Mad Hatter and the March Hare was not high on my list of priorities, but I went. It's called parenthood, folks. My little Jessie didn't ask to be born. Dance lessons were also my idea.

We got to the school auditorium half an hour before showtime, as instructed, but Jessie was not in makeup or costume. What's the half hour for, if not patting ribbons into place, rouging plump little cheeks, and applying mascara oh-so-carefully between rapid-fire blinks. When my tiny dancer pronounced herself satisfied with her greasepaint, I helped her locate the purple gauze scarf she needed for her second number and then trotted off to find a seat.

After settling myself in the middle of a center row halfway between the stage and the rear exits, I checked out the program for familiar names. Eagle River is small enough that you wind up knowing somebody just about everywhere you go. For me, that's the town's principal charm. Raising kids is easier in a small town because they grow up knowing where they fit in their community, feeling firmly rooted in nurturing soil. Which makes their eventual transplantation easier when they have to figure out later where they fit in the world at large. The program listed the standard tales and legends. With the exception of one dance, the recital consisted of interpretations of little girl favorites—*Hansel and Gretel, Sleeping Beauty, The Little Mermaid*—scored by Disney and the occasional Russian composer. The exception was an Athabascan classic telling how Raven reclaimed the sun and moon from an evil man and returned them to their rightful place in the sky. The music for the Raven tale was to be provided by a Native choral group, and the principal dancer was listed as Katya Doyon, niece of one friend and daughter of another.

Dropping the program to my lap, I craned around, scoping the auditorium from end to end, hoping to locate Belle or her brother among the rustling crowd of parents and other relatives. Apparently, I wasn't the only one eager to locate John Doyon. He'd made it only three steps inside the door to the auditorium before a wedge of shoulders had dammed the aisle in front, forcing him to exchange greetings and small talk with a dozen or more men and women with the ready smiles and outstretched hands of those who hope for an inside track. Usually that kind of grinning glad-hander looks right through a Native, but John Doyon is not your typical Athabascan. Never was, in fact. After taking top honors at the native boarding school in Sitka, he spurned the full scholarships offered by the Ivy League recruiters and went to the University of Alaska in Fairbanks to study development issues. He also won a seat in the state legislature.

He followed up his B.A. and first stint in Juneau with a law degree from Stanford, returning home in time to sign on to the team of a newly elected attorney general. When his man lost four years later, John finally said yes to the Ivy League and picked up an M.B.A. at Harvard. After which he started working for the Tanana Native Corporation and finally caught the attention of even the most myopic of white business types.

To understand John Doyon's sudden popularity, you must understand that Alaska's natives accomplished what no Indians in the Lower Forty-eight managed—winning the *war* as well as the battles. The key to their success was the Native Claims Settlement Act, engineered by savvy lawyers who withdrew the roadblocks preventing construction of the Trans-Alaska oil pipeline in exchange for forty million acres of land and one billion dollars in cash. At the same time, twelve regional corporations like TNC—Tanana Native Corporation—were created to manage the real estate and the money. Rotarians and Kiwanians want to shake John Doyon's hand because he's the chief executive officer of TNC, which is the largest private landowner in the USA, holding title to 12.5 million acres. TNC's nine thousand Native shareholders own nice chunks of Florida, Arizona, and Southern California, plus more labor-intensive ventures such as fishing fleets, canning plants, drilling rigs, and timber mills closer to home. All of which makes John Doyon a pretty popular guy, sort of an Alaskan version of Lee Iacocca or Frank Perdue without the commercials. With a balance sheet like TNC's, who needs advertising?

The lights started blinking before the glad-handers

relented and let John Doyon sit down. I'd managed to catch his eye with a high sign and waved him into a seat next to me. That set up a little buzz around us, though I'm not sure whether the cause was specific or general. Specific being speculation about the possibly flagrant admission of adultery by an eminence like John Doyon. General being visceral outrage at the possibility of any interracial pairing. Both possibilities had been raised between us and dismissed long ago.

Noticing his empty hands, I offered him my program. "How's Granny?"

He took the program and smiled gently. "Fine, fine. Eager to get home and begin the fishing."

Just then the lights dimmed, the curtains parted, and the performance began. First out thundered a herd of purple unicorns. The sequined tights encasing chubby three-year-old legs glittered under the stage lights, and the satin horns atop their heads bobbed in counterpoint. Their instructor came last, dressed seriously in a black long-sleeved leotard and calf-length skirt. After straightening the ragged line of unicorns, she led the herd through a few turns of creative movement—sweep arm, step, step, clap, clap; sweep arm, step, step, clap, clap. Camcorders whirred and 35mm cameras flashed as a sentimental sigh bestirred the crowd.

I glanced at John Doyon and caught him stifling a yawn. When I grinned, he tilted his head toward me. "Why aren't you yawning, Lauren? My pilot said you spent a couple of sleepless nights."

A flush of embarrassment heated my cheeks, and I wondered if he'd ever faced a grizzly. He must have sensed the question because he touched my elbow and nodded. "Only once. I was just a boy. I sang to him as I backed away. Later, I discovered I'd wet myself." He grinned. "Except for that, Belle and Granny wouldn't have believed my story."

A burst of applause signaled the end of the unicorn's dance. I joined the clapping. "You've been traveling, too?"

John nodded again. "Consulting work across the border—Bear Lake, Dogrib, Yellowknife. Soon their land claims will be settled. They can learn from our mistakes."

A stagehand pushed a yummy-looking gingerbread house into the center spotlight and was followed by a troupe of Hansels and Gretels in lederhosen and dirndl skirts who began a sprightly waltz. John and I spoke in whispers, continuing our hushed exchanges throughout the first act as class after class took to the stage, a charming parade whose dance proficiency increased with each offering. We'd covered a lot of ground by the time the lights came up for intermission. I'd forgotten that John Doyon liked Kirby Rogers, a fact I'd always put down to the parallels of their pro-development views. Kirby Rogers laid claim to more complexity than I'd imagined possible. The subtle undercurrent of hostility now tinging John's words indicated his attitude was far from simple as well. As the crowd got to its feet, John started to rise, but I grabbed his arm and held him in his seat. "Tell me again what you heard in Fort Norman."

For a moment he fixed his dark eyes on me. Then he shrugged and repeated the story. "An Inuk claimed to have seen flying polar bears and white men hunting on the ice in early spring. He was drunk and his story was wild."

I released his arm. "Did you believe him?"

John Doyon shrugged again. "Some did. Some said there were other hunts farther west. In the Yukon up beyond Keno. Those hunts guaranteed any prey— even the grizzly—for a price."

As carefully as my inner agitation allowed, I folded my hands into my lap. So that's what it came down to. Money. How typical of *Scumbag americanus*. "Did you believe that story?"

He sighed. "There is always some truth in these tales. To me, the meaning is clear—someone is providing big game hunts with guaranteed results."

"Bringing the prey to the predator would be simple enough for anyone with three things: tranquilizers, transportation, and a steady source of game." Warming to his subject, he settled back against the seat, showing the heritage of his Russian grandfather in his enjoyment of the opportunity to prove his intelligence. "Obviously, the last can be very difficult because most big game is protected. And locating animals of even the most abundant varieties can be difficult, unless you know where to look."

"Most Alaskans know where to look for grizzly bears—the McNeil River Game Sanctuary." I narrowed my eyes in John's direction. "Kirby Rogers certainly does."

For the first time I saw an overt sign of hostility in the flash of his dark eyes. "What you're suggesting is nonsense. And speculation of the grossest sort."

I didn't flinch under his gaze. "Roland Taft was my friend. He said there were bears missing from McNeil."

Again his eyes flashed fire. "Kirby Rogers is my friend. He is loyal in word and deed."

I leaned closer, almost hissing now. "He is a man who mows down wolves with automatic weapons on helo-hunts."

His eyes hardened. "If you had your way, the animals would have free passage while my people starve."

I blinked back tears, too stung for words. An unwilling peace was declared by the start of the second act. John's daughter danced brilliantly as the Raven. My daughter showed true promise amid the swirling rainbow of scarves. And all the while, I was trapped in a circle of what John Doyon called speculation. I called it facts.

Kirby Rogers had the tools and the talent—animal tranquilizers, helicopters, and intimate knowledge of the bears. Adding those three facts to the impressions of a helicopter's skids found near the cabin, I now had a suspect and a motive. But what was the crime—the theft of some grizzlies or the killing of Roland Taft?

14

Every Saturday my home doubles as a pancake house, but, fortunately, the next day Travis MacDonald arrived early enough to do the honors. Most Saturday mornings he does, which means I can't sleep in or roam around looking like a slob unless I'm ready to have my mothering called into question. Not by Travis, you understand. My kids are the hard cases. Jessie thinks it's perfectly awful for any mom to snooze later than her kids. Jake insists that I embarrass him when I neglect to comb my hair or apply mascara. Before you dismiss my children as smart-mouth brats, cast your mind back to days of yore. Remember when Mom or Dad said/did/wore something that left you perfectly mortified in front of those wonderful pals whose names you can't remember anymore? I most certainly do, so I give my kids a break. Meaning I'd pulled on a pair of old jeans and one of Max's Oxford cloth shirts, secured my hair behind a fake tortoiseshell headband, and given my eyes a triple dose of Almay lash-lengthening black before Travis arrived.

He elbowed through the door, big and brown with red hair textured like wire and knuckly hands that grasped a bag of breakfast goodies. "Blueberry pancakes coming up. First berries of the season, fresh from somewhere. And just squoozed orange juice, fresh from Safeway."

I took the groceries and nodded toward the mug of coffee I had poured when I saw his pickup pull into the drive. "And for the chef, French Roast."

From her perch on a stool at the counter, Nina paused between bites of a bagel to add a hearty slug of Jack Daniel's to his mug. "With just a little snort."

Travis grinned as he ambled loose-jointed to his reward. "Ah, ladies, you do make a man feel welcome." He sipped his coffee, closing his eyes as he savored the brew. "And you're the only women north of Dawson Creek can make coffee worth a damn."

That said, he got down to work, pulling a clean chef's apron from the linen drawer and a big glass mixing bowl from the cupboard. No Bisquick for this guy. Measuring by eye, he added flour, sugar, salt, and baking powder to the bowl and swirled it around to mix while the microwave melted a pat of butter. When the microwave beeped, he dumped in eggs, milk, butter, and his secret ingredient—vanilla. Then he stirred everything up, careful not to overbeat. When the consistency of the batter finally met his approval, Trav again had time to talk. He started with a longstanding gripe.

"Kids glued to cartoons again?" He glared in the direction of the family room, where some vacuous animated characters held my children in thrall. "Lauren, I simply don't understand why you permit that. You're usually so sensible."

This from a man who insists on paying cash—with greenbacks, never checks—and refuses to own a credit card, even for convenience. I couldn't rouse much enthusiasm for my usual argument. "One morning a week, Travis. For three hours max."

"Still." He popped five plates into a warm oven. "No good will come of it."

Nina smothered her amusement with a hand across her lips, but I couldn't swallow my bark of laughter. "You sound just like somebody's Aunt Minnie." When his glare started to soften, I redirected his attention onto a safer topic. "What's the scoop on your rogue pilot?"

He adjusted the flame under the griddle. "Don't have much. Probably flying a Super Cub, but who isn't?" He poured a dollop of vegetable oil on the griddle and spread it with a paper towel. "Pilot may be a woman. At least, that's what one fellow says."

Locating one rogue pilot sounds like a simple task. Not in Anchorage, a town which at last count had six airports within the city limits, not including the many lakes that easily accommodate floatplanes. Don't even mention helicopters. Visitors to our fair city express amazement at discovering that whenever the eyes lift skyward a fair number of aircraft may be seen buzzing about overhead. The heavy traffic in the skies above Anchorage gives ulcers to those who man the control towers, most of whom say daily prayers that they'll be off-duty when the inevitable major crash occurs. Juneau holds the air disaster record in Alaska for the mountain-side crash of a Boeing 727 in 1971 that killed 111 people. So far, Anchorage has been spared a major catastrophe. Even so, Alaska's loss of countless small planes has spread tentacles of tragedy throughout the city, state, and nation. Just ask former Congresswoman Lindsy Boggs of Louisiana. Or me.

The kids ate on trays in front of the television while Travis, Nina, and I stayed in the kitchen, safely out of hearing range of the strident cartoon bedlam. After the meal the chef relaxed with a parting cup of coffee, and Nina gathered her softball gear while I did the dishes and cleaned up the kitchen. When Nina's ride tooted outside and carried her away, Trav rinsed out his mug and rousted Jake from the couch. No sooner had they left than Jessie lost interest in Saturday morning TV and decided to whine at Mom for a while. "I'm bored. There's nothing to do. Everybody 'cept me has something to do today."

She was right. I'd planned to get my hands dirty in the garden, simultaneously freeing the vegetables of weeds and my mind of extraneous thoughts so I could figure out the next step in unearthing the solution to Roland's death. However, last night didn't really add up to much in the mother love column. Not with Jessie backstage or onstage and me fretting and fuming next to John Doyon in the audience. I remembered to get her an ice cream treat after the performance but was so distracted by my tiff with John that I barely managed the necessary praise for her accomplishment.

Deciding to do better today, I dropped to my knees in front of her. "We can do anything you want, sweetheart." I brushed a kiss over her baby-soft lips. "Just name it. We've got all day."

"I wanna go swimming." Her brown eyes glowed,

and her slim body vibrated with excitement. "At Mirror Lake!"

I bit back the refusal that automatically rose to my lips. After all, I did say anything, even if the day's high was unlikely to reach sixty-five degrees. "Okay, babe. You get our stuff together. It may be cold, so pack our polar fleece."

Jessie spun on a heel, darted to the door, and then stopped and turned back toward me. "Should I bring that sun stuff we used in Hawaii?"

Sunscreen. Didn't I wish! I shook my head. "No way. Let's get brown if we can."

I'd dirtied the kitchen again fixing a picnic of tunafish sandwiches, Doritos, cookies, and fruit when the phone rang. I grabbed it before the machine answered and wedged the receiver between chin and shoulder. "Hello."

"Mrs. Maxwell?" The question came hushed and breathy to my ear. "Mrs. Lauren Maxwell?"

"Speaking." Annoyance sharpened my voice. I hate being called Mrs. Maxwell. "Who is this, please?"

"You don't know me. Not really. But I have some information you might be interested in."

I took a deep breath and let it out slowly, trying for patience. You wouldn't believe how often people try this cloak-and-dagger nonsense on me. In my line of work hardly anybody is ever in danger, unless you count other species. Still, it wouldn't do to frighten her off. "What kind of information?"

"Information about Roland Taft. And the man who murdered him."

That grabbed me. For a long moment I stood there with my mouth hanging open. *Murder*. Somebody had finally said the word I'd been unable to pronounce.

The caller's audacity gave me the courage I needed to test the informant and run the risk of scaring her off. "You say you've got information. Fine. Suppose you give me a reason to believe. Like maybe telling me *why* Roland had to die?"

"Because he'd figured it out." Impatient now. Maybe ready to bolt. "Because Roland figured out that bears were being taken."

And there it was—confirmation of my worst suspicions. Anonymous confirmation that had to get on the record somehow. Or else Kirby Rogers would get away with it! "You've convinced me." My voice sounded kind of shaky. "But to convince others, I've got to have evidence. Names, dates, documents."

The caller didn't miss a beat. "I've got everything you need. When can we meet?"

Just then, Jessie bounced back into the kitchen, her dance bag stuffed to bursting with everything we needed for a chilly day at the beach. She dropped the bag at my feet and stood there with folded arms, just to make sure I knew she was waiting.

I thought fast, but the caller didn't like my plan. Something about her mother. Finally she agreed to meet me at Mirror Lake at noon. She'd know me on sight. Maybe I'd recognize her, as well.

Ninety minutes later I spotted her picking her way across the beach. Kirby Rogers's assistant—what was her name? The woman Vanessa Larrabee called creepy. At the time I'd dismissed that description and settled for one of my own—drab. In one way the briefcase tucked under her arm added the final ludicrous detail to her obvious discomfort. A crowd of whooping youngsters tore past her, splitting neatly into two streams that left her spinning in their wake.

In another way the briefcase added a creepy touch. After all, the woman's purpose was serious disloyalty to her boss. No matter how richly Kirby Rogers deserved unmasking, a taint of dishonor still clings to squealers.

I got to my feet as she approached and stuck out my hand. "I'm afraid I've forgotten your name."

She glanced over each shoulder before replying. "I'm Julianne Blanchard, Mrs. Maxwell." She gave me a limp hand. "I don't have much time. There's no one to help on weekends, and Mother can't be left for long."

Folding myself onto the towel abandoned by Jess, I offered her my sand chair. "Is it just the two of you?"

She nodded, hunching over the briefcase she'd laid across her knees. "Yes. Mother's a victim of MS, you see. She's bedridden and requires total care. Which is why I never said anything before." Her eyes glistened. Tears? "Even when Roland practically begged, I was afraid I'd lose my job. No one likes a whistle-blower. No one."

Right then I decided to try. I'm a closet elitist about lots of things—looks, brains, talent. Not something I'm proud of. So what if Julianne Blanchard was a mousy little careerist? She was also a human being. A pretty fine one, by the looks of it. How many women in their prime saddle themselves with a crippled parent? How many mid-level bureaucrats risk their retirement to expose wrongdoing by higher-ups?

I touched the sleeve of her navy windbreaker. "I do. I'm sure you're scared to death, but bringing Kirby Rogers justice is the right thing to do."

"Roland wasn't afraid." She blinked her eyes and shuddered. "Look what happened to him."

I patted her arm. "You'll be safe, I promise." I was determined to deliver on that promise. "I'll keep anything you say absolutely confidential until he's locked up where he belongs."

She gave me a little smile and pulled a manila envelope from her briefcase. "It's all here. All the documents you'll need."

For a second I weighed the envelope in my hand, wishing for greater bulk. Then I set it aside and raised my eyes to Julianne Blanchard. "Tell me what you have."

"There's Roland's letter, telling about two dates when he noticed a mysterious helicopter in the McNeil River area." She ticked the evidence off on her fingers. "There's a state aircraft log showing that Kirby Rogers checked out helicopters on both dates. And flight manifests."

Three raised fingers—one for each document. Her hand curled into a fist, and she leaned toward me, lowering her voice. "Both manifests show triple the mileage needed to fly round-trip to his listed destination. Mileage that's the exact distance to McNeil River."

Grinning, she sat back. "Exact."

Documents don't necessarily prove anything. At best, this was circumstantial evidence. I allowed myself a little frown. "Coincidence, Kirby could say. So why kill Roland? Explain that. If Kirby'd stopped right then, nobody would have been able to prove anything."

A flash of something in her eyes. Anger? Impatience? "Because Roland was right about his paper. Kirby's statistics were made up. Pretty soon everybody will know that."

Julianne leaned forward again and tapped the envelope lying next to her feet. "I'll tell you what's not in here. The aircraft log for the day Roland Taft died."

A rush of color painted her pale cheeks pink. "Kirby Rogers flew that day. I should know. I ordered the helicopter first thing that morning. Three days later you found Roland's body."

Tap, tap, tap—her finger beat against the envelope between us. "What I can't explain is why no record of that trip appears in the log."

15

Persuading Julianne Blanchard to rat on her boss took plenty of coaxing. She didn't try to hide her hatred of Kirby Rogers. Whenever she mentioned him, her eyes flashed fire and her lip curled under a snarl, the first bit of spirit I'd seen in her. Outside of one or two brief glimpses, mousy timidity remained her usual mode. She *couldn't* risk losing her job. Mother *needed* her. Everyone *hated* informers. All of which I acknowledged while hammering home my own set of justifications. Roland Taft was *dead*. Kirby Rogers continued to *loot* the wilderness. Justice *must* prevail. Back and forth we went, a seesaw argument that filled our hour at Mirror Lake and two subsequent meetings. Finally Julianne Blanchard relented and agreed to telephone me the next time her boss seemed ready to go grizzly grabbing. I'd decided early on that catching Kirby Rogers in the act was the only way that justice had the slightest chance of prevailing.

One good thing came of my lengthy negotiations

with Julianne—I'd learned a lot about Kirby Rogers's methods. Turned out that she never suspected him of anything worse than rabid resource exploitation until Roland Taft's letter arrived and revealed the presence of a mysterious helicopter in the McNeil River area. She tucked Roland's letter into a locked drawer until she could give the matter some thought. When she had, she realized her boss was the likely pilot of the mystery helicopter but still didn't know why he'd gone to such trouble to disguise his destination on those dates. Like good lawyers and good bureaucrats, Julianne had learned not to ask a question unless she already knew the answer. So she kept Roland's letter locked in a drawer and kept quiet, awaiting further developments. Not until after Roland's death, when I turned up asking about missing bears, did she put it all together. And in such a way that I could with reasonable certainty have advance notice the next time Kirby Rogers did one of his dirty deals at the McNeil River sanctuary.

Humans are creatures of habit and followers of routine. Julianne had backtracked until she figured out Kirby Rogers's routine. In the days before his mystery flights, he always received a series of brief long-distance calls that didn't seem to concern department business. She knew that because in an effort to assess the efficiency of ADF&G managers, the bean counters in Juneau had decreed that all phone calls should be logged. Julianne's snooping revealed that Kirby's spate of long-distance calls were not included in his telephone log. And, it turned out, Kirby Rogers didn't break another routine, even when intent on perfidy. Or murder. Julianne Blanchard *always* reserved his aircraft, usually a day in advance. How like a man to insist on his privileges, even when doing dirt! The next time her boss reserved a helicopter after receiving a series of brief long-distance calls, my informant promised to notify me at once. Because the next time Kirby Rogers went hunting for bear, I intended to beat him to McNeil River.

"And do what?" Boyce Reade's question echoed the one I'd been asking myself for days. Of course, I didn't telephone my boss at our D.C. headquarters until I had the answer. "Videotaping a theft smacks of grandstanding, Lauren. And that is certain to alienate what few friends we have at Alaska's natural resource agencies."

Closing my eyes, I imagined his, as cool and gray as a rainy day. I shivered and let the image dissolve as I straightened my spine. "You've got to trust me on this, Boyce. It's the only way. This guy's got real clout. He's got the power structure wired—private, public, and native. If we don't nail him on tape, Kirby Rogers will walk. Guaranteed."

Doubt tickled my throat, but I refused to give it voice. So what if I hadn't mentioned to Boyce my suspicions that Kirby Rogers had something to do with Roland's death? I still couldn't bring myself to say murder. Who in her right mind could? Even Julianne Blanchard had no explanation of how Kirby Rogers might have contrived Roland's death. Her strong conviction that he had was based on nothing more solid than gut instinct. Proving him guilty of Roland's murder would fall to the law enforcement types who'd move in on Kirby Rogers once I'd showed them my tape of the theft of a grizzly at McNeil River. After the high drama of that revelation, my imagination went sort of fuzzy on details. And one's own fuzzy thinking is not a topic one raises with one's boss. Not if one values continued employment, one doesn't.

Across a zillion miles of space and telephone wires, Boyce sighed into my ear. "All right, Lauren. I'll trust you on this. But don't let me down."

After I gave him my solemn promise, Boyce asked for an update on my search for new data that could torpedo the federal government's plans to allow drilling in the Arctic National Wildlife Refuge.

"There's plenty of data, but we can't get to it. The science on the *Exxon Valdez* spill is certain to be damning—when it's made public." It was my turn to sigh. "The judge's gag order on that information will stay in effect until all civil and criminal cases are settled. Exxon and the state want a settlement, but the coastal natives aren't buying. Their subsistence food sources are wiped out, and they want justice."

"Hmmm." I pictured his brow wrinkling under the weight of his thoughts. "Any chance anecdotal evidence from the natives will add up to anything?"

I laughed. "You tell me, boss. How much weight do the bigshots inside the beltway give to the concerns of poor people who aren't white?"

Boyce didn't bother to answer, so I went on. "What are the chances of using the gag order itself as a roadblock to drilling? You know—*the administration's short-sightedness dangerously compounded by the failure to consider scientific evidence which would show blah, blah, blah?*"

"Blah, blah, blah?" He laughed lightly. "I suppose that might work. If we had the specifics of blah, blah, blah."

My heart tripped into a faster beat. Tit for tat.

Boyce would let me grandstand but only if I delivered the goods on the Arctic refuge. "I'll try. You may have to settle for abstracts."

"Abstracts will be fine." His voice carried a smile now. "And I'll have our legal people look into that suggestion of yours. Good angle, Lauren. Nice work."

The glow from Boyce's praise almost lasted through the afternoon I spent prowling for information at ADF&G, but as the horror stories accumulated, cold rage finally overwhelmed the diminishing warmth. I started with the commercial fishery people, hitting paydirt right off when I ran across a young woman whose home village was thoroughly oiled.

"The elders suffer worst." Deborah Komkoff swirled the tea bag in her mug. "They got none of the cleanup money and are forced to eat town meat. The mussels are few and many have sores. Seals are also scarce. They look at the liver and don't eat the spotty ones. Most have spots."

Subsistence doesn't work if the game is gone. Rural Alaskans eat 443 pounds of wild meat, fowl, fish, and berries each year. The average American each year buys 255 pounds of equivalent products at the supermarket, devouring steroids and pesticides along with their meat. The Alaskan fight for survival used to be easiest on the coast, where natives found abundant populations of seals and sea lions, clams and mussels, deer and otter. Most coastal villages never knew hunger. The *Exxon Valdez* changed all that, oiling the beaches and sea that were the native's lifeblood, offering a temporary bonanza of cleanup pay that bought cars and boats and satellite dishes. And town meat.

I made sympathetic noises as Deborah Komkoff

continued. "I just worked on eggs. Things are getting better. This year, for pink salmon, oiled areas have only 50 percent greater mortality than non-oiled. But growth rates are down in all species. And for herring we have huge increases in abnormalities in embryos and larvae."

She passed me a sheaf of papers—more than an abstract—and suggested I drop in on a friend of hers in the habitat division. John Richardson turned out to be very young, very bright, and very angry.

"Before the *Exxon Valdez,* everything was speculation. Our water is pretty cold. We thought that would slow down recovery." He frowned. "Not that recovery is ever fast. We knew from a spill on Cape Cod that intertidal areas hadn't recovered a decade later. A Nova Scotia spill showed significant die-offs of benthic plants and animals with little recovery in six years. The *Amoco Cadiz* showed that oil trapped in the water column just wipes out subtidal organisms. Based on that knowledge, we speculated that things would be worse here."

He smacked a hand on his desk. "Well, now we know. Oil concentrations in bottom-dwelling fish have not declined since the spill. The contamination of sediments in some places goes three hundred feet deep, continuing the exposure of intertidal and subtidal organisms. In turn, those clams and other invertebrates contaminate otters and shore-dwelling wildlife that forage the beaches."

Translation: Oil breaks down slowly in cold water, and the reality of the food chain means that the oil in the water eventually winds up on land, contaminating eagles, bears, deer, mink, otters, and literally hundreds of thousands of migrating birds. I asked John

Richardson when he thought things would start to get better.

"Better? You've got to be kidding." He shook his head. "My best guess is that things are going to get much, much worse. When terrestrial mammals start dying in significant numbers, maybe people on the outside will start to care."

He was right, of course. With the exception of wildlife biologists, who gets choked up over the destruction of herring larvae or pink salmon eggs? Dead grizzly bears and bald eagles are something else entirely. And we can't afford to lose many because we're sparsely populated, wildlife-wise. Although Alaska is nearly four times larger than California, we have 155,000 moose compared to 800,000 deer in the Golden State. Our hunters took 68,000 ducks in 1988. Californians killed 464,000. With numbers like that to begin with, absorbing a poisonous spill like the *Exxon Valdez* risks catastrophic population crashes of land animals. But the predicted die-off of terrestrial animals wouldn't come soon enough to save the Arctic National Wildlife Refuge. Maybe the preliminary findings in the research papers John Richardson gave me would.

Buoyed with that hope, I continued to troll the hallways of ADF&G, hoping to lure more angry and outraged employees into risking their jobs to get the truth out. The next person at risk turned out to be me, however, because around the corner I ran into Kirby Rogers. He was one of a trio of men so deep into a kibitz that I almost snuck right by. Unfortunately, good-looking guys like Kirby have special antennae where women are concerned, and his picked me up.

"Lauren!" Excusing himself in a hurry, he started after me. "Lauren, please wait!"

The please got to me. I spun on my heel, still moving but walking backward now. "Hello, Kirby. I'm in a real hurry."

He trotted up, brown eyes all agleam with warmth. "I've been meaning to call you. I'm sorry about what I said."

That stopped me cold. An apology? Was he ready to admit that he'd been wrong about Roland? Was he ready to confess that he'd fudged the numbers in his bear paper?

"Not that it wasn't the truth." His long fingers circled my arm. "But I could have handled it better. I know Taft was a good friend of yours. In fact, I think that's what set me off. After finally meeting you, I was kind of jealous."

The King of the Schmoozers was at it again, sweeping me off my feet. I swear I could have identified a set of his fingerprints just from the touch of his hand on my arm. He'd loosened his tie and unbuttoned his collar, exposing a lean length of neck that invited nuzzling. I might have lost it completely and swayed against him to get started, if only he hadn't opened his mouth again. The repetition saved me. The second time he slandered Roland Taft, his words finally sunk in.

"Taft might have been nuts." He smiled down at me. "But he had great taste in women."

I yanked my arm free. "You're the one who's nuts, Rogers." I backed off a foot. "I looked into your theory about Roland. I searched his cabin and found nothing to support it. And I talked to three of the top people in bear biology and not one of them agreed with you."

He frowned and took a step forward, hand reaching for me again.

Suddenly I felt exposed and vulnerable. If Julianne Blanchard was right, this man had killed Roland Taft. So why in God's name was I telling him that I'd started to demolish the safe haven he'd built with his lies?

His fingers brushed my skin again. "Lauren, I—"

Terror galvanized me. With a mighty leap, I jumped beyond his reach. Beyond his touch. Surprise widened those gorgeous eyes and moved that marvelous mouth to speech. Before either could have any effect, I turned on my heel and darted away.

16

The trap I'd laid for Kirby Rogers almost didn't get sprung. As soon as Julianne Blanchard alerted me to his imminent departure for McNeil River, I tried to arrange my own and found myself grounded. Cal Williamson's damned boycott was still on. No pilot in southeast Alaska was "available" to fly me to the game sanctuary. My scheme to nail Kirby Rogers had revealed the first glitch in my planning. More revelations—and glitches—would follow. Lots of them.

The second Wednesday in June dawned at 4:16 A.M. Julianne's call came just after ten. Nina had dropped the kids with friends on her way to the clinic, so I had the house to myself. The kitchen counter was littered with a month's worth of glossy grocery inserts from the Sunday paper. I was sipping my second cup of coffee and snipping cents-off coupons when the phone rang. My informant sounded even more breathless than usual.

"He's been on the phone all morning." Pant, pant, pant. "Now he wants a helicopter for tomorrow." Pant, pant, pant. "He's leaving at first light."

"Okay, okay. Let me think a second." My heart pounded as if I'd run a four-minute mile, but I resisted the urge to pant in turn. "So he got a bunch of long-distance calls. You checked his phone log, right?"

"Right." Her voice went military, all salutes and yessirs. "When he stepped out of his office, I checked his log. No notations since yesterday."

"So now he wants a helicopter. And you reserved one, right?"

"Right. First the calls, then the aircraft. That's the pattern."

"Okay, then." The surge of adrenalin had left my knees weak. I sank against a stool. "I'll take it from here, Julianne. Thanks for coming through for me."

She didn't want to let me go so quickly. I endured the obligatory pleas to be careful and anxious warnings about our quarry's cunning. When she started in with questions about specific details of my plans, I tried to shoo her without giving the appearance of a brush-off. "I'll fly in. And I better get going because there's a million things to do."

"You're sure you'll be okay? Do you have a reservation?"

I sighed heavily. How could I have a reservation when I didn't know when I'd be going? "No reservation required. Pilots are easy to find."

Except when they aren't. And that day pilots definitely were not to be found. Not, at least, by me. That was apparent from a half dozen phone calls to air services where the cheery voice on the other end of the line turned chill as soon as I identified myself. Which left me with an excruciating dilemma—from whom to bum a ride, Travis MacDonald or John Doyon?

I'd never flown with Travis, which was a deliberate choice I made not long after he entered our lives. The fact that he'd led the search for Max meant that any flight I took with him would be fraught with all kinds of significance. Plus he would have me at his mercy for another of his interminable lectures on the irrationality of my obstinate refusal to let Jake fly. And then there was my fear of letting Travis get any closer, a fear stimulated by the certainty that my son needed him a lot more than I did. Some sparks must be snuffed out without acknowledgment.

So I swallowed my pride and called John Doyon, defender of Kirby Rogers and possessor of a fleet of aircraft. After fighting my way through a thicket of gatekeepers determined to spare the CEO of Tanana Native Corporation from unnecessary distractions, the man himself came on the line. We batted pleasantries back and forth, neither mentioning our last exchange, and then, without explanation, I asked for a ride to the McNeil River area. John put me on hold while he called around to see what was available and came back with the offer of a chopper ferrying building materials to a tourist lodge under construction near Iliamna. I'd have to be in Homer by six P.M. to catch the last flight.

"Sounds great, John." I kept my voice brisk, hoping to get off the phone quickly. "Thanks."

The busy executive wasn't letting me off that easy. "Again to McNeil. Who's going with you?"

"No one." I didn't leave any room for his logical

question or my logical fears. "No need. Plenty of people around at this time of year. I'll be all right."

"Not so many people until July. Not so many bears, either." He paused, then gave in to the Cassandra lurking inside every human. "You'll be fine. Remember to sing softly and back away slowly and you'll be fine."

Nobody believed Cassandra and I didn't believe him. For days I'd been in a state of absolute denial, refusing to face what my decision to trap Kirby Rogers inevitably meant. I was going back to bear country. Alone this time. Back to the land of four-inch claws and one-swipe killing power, of incisors that tore flesh and speed that could outrun a horse. *Alone.*

Terror, more than anything, explained my hysteria at the next glitch that appeared. I couldn't find my Sierra cup. I'd been packed for days, just like a commonsensical woman expecting her first child. A month before Jake's birth I'd packed my hospital bag—lollipops for labor, wool socks for delivery, and champagne for later. A week before Julianne's call, I'd packed my McNeil gear—a camcorder for Kirby, a .45 Colt for the bears, and extra cartridges for me. As for the missing Sierra cup, what began as a minor inconvenience soon loomed large in my imagination. How could I go camping without my Sierra cup? What would I drink with? Heat my soup in? Eat my cereal from? Talk about obsessing! My eyes teared at the thought that the cup which once touched Max's lips was gone forever. I sobbed at the memory of bathing the infant Jake by dipping water with the lost cup. I positively squalled at the realization that Jessie would not inherit the cup given me by my mother on the first day of Girl Scout camp. *Maudlin* is the only word for my behavior. And fear of bears the only explanation. A fear I wound up expressing through my absolutely bonkers obsession with the loss of a stupid tin cup.

After packing the 4-Runner and advising Nina of my departure, I headed for Homer. On the way I swung by Pay'N Save and picked up a new Sierra cup. In the parking lot outside, I tested it in my hand. Free of dents and memories, the cup shone in the late morning sun, a round and shallow bowl with a wire handle easily hung from a belt. Positively utilitarian and certainly nothing to cry over.

The next glitch appeared when I was airborne over Kachemak Bay. The *whuppa-whuppa-whuppa* of the rotors on the TNC helicopter made conversation difficult, but the pilot was a gregarious young fellow determined to try. Right after takeoff, the radio started squawking, and for a while he barked back. When the Homer Spit had fallen away behind us and the cone of Augustine Island had begun rising from the sea ahead, the radio finally fell silent. The pilot yanked the communication rig from his head, snarling it in his long dark hair, and grinned at me. "Why you want to go visiting McNeil when there's nobody home? Gonna be lonely over there."

"There's people around." I tried for a reassuring smile. "The permit visitors don't arrive till July, but the guides are already in camp."

"No, ma'am, they aren't." His grin widened, and he shook his shaggy head. "Flew out yesterday for a little R and R before the season starts. They'll be back next week. Looks like you're on your own."

That news soured my stomach in a hurry. Not that

I'd been counting on the ADF&G guys at McNeil River for help. Far from it, in fact. I'd planned to avoid them at all costs, figuring Kirby Rogers certainly would. The touristos stick to the barren tundra near the falls at the mouth of the river, a locale that offers virtually no cover for grizzly grabbers. I'd worked it out in my head that Rogers must do his dirty work farther upstream, where thickets of scrub spruce and alder offered sufficient screening. I'd figured on being set down on the beach where I'd landed with Belle Doyon and then force marching to the area I'd decided must be the right place. I didn't expect any trouble because I planned only to videotape Kirby Rogers, not confront him. Only a fool would confront a man who'd already killed to protect his secret. But deep down I guess I'd counted on the ADF&G guides in the camp by the beach to save my bacon if anything went wrong. Knowing they'd flown out changed everything, including my plan.

I cocked an eyebrow at the grinning pilot and shrugged. "That's okay. I'm used to being alone. I've been on my own for a lot of years."

The rest of the flight I spent revising my plan. First off, I figured Kirby Rogers had ordered his guides out of McNeil. In another few weeks ten lucky tourists whose names had been selected by lottery would be allowed to view the grizzlies at McNeil Falls each day, a parade of visitors that continued right through the summer. There'd be plenty of other visitors in the area as well—backpackers, fishermen, you name it. With that upcoming population boom, this would probably be Kirby's last opportunity for months to take a grizzly. I reasoned that he'd shooed away the guides who were potential witnesses so he'd have an easier time finding a bear to grab. Mid-June might be too soon for the salmon and most bears to return to the river, but a couple of grizzlies could always be counted on to show up early. And when the early birds arrived, they'd head straight for the falls on McNeil River. So would I.

Augustine Island's volcanic cone loomed on my right as Kamishak Bay opened before us. I touched the pilot's arm to get his attention. "Put me down near the camp on the beach at McNeil Cove."

He nodded and then glanced at me. "When do you want to be picked up?"

"Maybe tomorrow, maybe the day after. Late." A gust of wind rocked the helicopter, and I grabbed my seat for support. "What time do you figure you can get here?"

"You name it. I'm just going back and forth, back and forth, flying mostly a ways north." He rocked his head from side to side. "How about you start a signal fire on the beach? I could see that way off."

Off-shore breezes rocked the helicopter as the TNC pilot set it down on the stony beach a dozen yards past the cabin where I'd spent the night after finding Roland's body. Unloading took no time at all. I grabbed my backpack, then ducked my head and ran clear of the rotors. The pilot's eternal grin widened yet again, and he gave me a thumbs-up before lifting off, hovering for a time and then swooping away to the north, quickly gaining elevation as the helicopter soared above the mouth of the McNeil River. Within minutes the sound of his engines died away, leaving me the lone intruder in the vast quiet of the great land.

I allowed myself to think about my kids just then and to wonder whether I was out of my mind. I refused to let Jake fly because of a morbid fear of losing him as I'd lost Max. But what about my son's fear of losing me? What about the possibility that Jake and Jessie Maxwell might end up orphans? That wasn't a nightmare scenario for my kids but a very real possibility. One parent down and one to go. And the one they had left hopped aboard any aircraft headed in the right direction, hung out in locales known to be frequented by man-killing beasts, and single-handedly took on known murderers. For what?

The answer to my question suddenly appeared a hundred yards offshore, lit by a triangle of golden light that streamed through a chink in the heavy cloud cover. The pod of whales announced its presence by blowing, spout after spout erupting across the waters of McNeil Cove. I counted five blows, each rising like an eight-foot balloon of vapor. A set of flukes lifted from the water—deeply notched in the center and scalloped on the rear margin. Humpbacks. Their paths laced silver seams in the calm water. And then one of the whales breached, heaving its mighty bulk into the air, sea water streaming from its barnacle-encrusted hide before it landed again with a terrific splash.

A torrent of joy streamed through me as the water exploded again and again, each time releasing that enormous creature who fell back to the sea to spin and roll and leap beyond his element again. As I watched the acrobatic display, my heart took flight. Not with the warm fuzzy-wuzzies of the nitwit naturalists, but with a sense of rightness about the world and my place in it.

In my world there is a place in the sea for whales and a place on the land for grizzlies. For I know with dead certainty that if there is no room on this earth for the wild, then there is no place on this planet for me.

17

The miraculous appearance of those humpbacks saved me from acting like an idiot. I had been eyeing the driftwood carefully piled in the lee of a cabin and seriously considering starting my signal fire two days early. Would any mother in her right mind consciously risk orphaning her babies? With the exception of the unlucky few whose self-sacrifice ensures the immediate survival of their offspring, forget it. And my Jake and my Jessie no longer had any parents to spare. Such were my thoughts as I stood on the beach at McNeil Cove in the slanting pre-solstice light of that June evening.

Don't I wish! My thoughts were hardly so selfless. Were, in fact, quite chaotic, shredded by four-inch claws and ripped by gnashing incisors. Remember fight or flight? I was getting ready to run, psyching myself up for the big skedaddle, preparing to scram. Self-preservation is basic to all species—a biological imperative—even if the alcohol haze and greed frenzy

of postindustrial America belies that fact. Biological-
ly, the kids don't count for much. What really counts
is the self, that random configuration of genetic codes
that makes each of us unique. Fundamental to all
animals is the drive to preserve that unique genetic
inheritance. Which is why starving animals often eat
their young. You can always have more offspring. But
as Madison Avenue and the soaps so aptly put it—
each of us has only one life to live.

Then the humpback breached and my humanity
resurfaced, battling down the dark primitive fears
with the clear light of reason. I stood looking out to
sea long after the pod swam out of view, leaving
behind a lacework of silver trails that finally lingered
only in memory. Max used to say that any idiot can
fight, but it takes brains to get along, and he was right.
Aggression comes down to us from our animal ancestors. Our humanity resides in our intelligence, which
is still evolving toward whatever pinnacle our species
may reach.

I hefted the backpack onto my shoulders and adjusted the straps for comfort, coolly appraising the
odds of having a fatal encounter with a grizzly. Not
likely, since I was forewarned and well armed in the
vicinity of bears pacified by habituation to humans.
Roland's death was rendered irrelevant by the possible involvement of Kirby Rogers and the elimination
of the bear that killed him. The brief darkness of a
subarctic summer night radically reduced the chances
of my stumbling across a bear unawares and vice
versa, particularly since I'd brought along my little
temple bell and planned to stay up all night ringing it.
As I started up the beach to the path that wound
across the Mikfik sedge flats, I began a chant modeled

on the Ghostbusters' theme song: "I ain't afraid of no bear!"

The walk got my heart pumping. I counterpointed the chant with deep breathing, figuring that in a pinch increased blood oxygenation never hurts. I also tried to remember the few simple rules McNeil River guides had devised over the past twenty years, successful rules that resulted in no deaths of bears or humans at the sanctuary. Always use the main trail to the falls. Stay in the viewing area. When meeting a bear, either go around or wait for the grizzly to move off. Like all species, brown bears have two choices when confronting danger—fight or flight. Getting too close can stress a grizzly into making the wrong choice. Experience showed that keeping one's distance and one's cool enhanced one's safety around bears. Unfortunately, I had no choice but to break one of the safety rules.

The path topped a low rise, providing an expansive look at the sedge flats and rolling alder-clad hills that embrace the McNeil River. I paused and scanned for bears, wishing I could set up my camera in the viewing area. Most of the good grizzly photos are shot from there. Wildlife photographers were among the first to recognize the peerless opportunity for bear-human interaction offered by the grizzly's annual migration to the falls. Those shooters homesteaded the present viewing area, setting up shop on a low knoll overlooking the falls. The consistent human use of the spot contributes to the safety of people and bears. Today the McNeil bears expected to see humans on the main trail or in the viewing area. Period. Too bad the absolute lack of cover meant I had to retreat into alder brush further upstream. The choice between risking a confrontation with a brown bear or a confrontation with Kirby Rogers turned out to be no contest. I'd take the grizzlies every time. After all, the deadliest species on earth is *Homo sapiens,* which in *Scumbag americanus* finds its most dangerous form.

The trail I followed was one of many converging on the falls like the spokes of a bicycle wheel. I crossed the entire expanse of the Mikfik sedge flats without seeing a bear. That surprised me, since the plant's early growth provides a protein-rich forage for winter-starved grizzlies. Although the highest concentration of bear in the area comes with the salmon runs of July and August, the McNeil sanctuary is the favored year-round range for a handful of individual animals, a fact evidenced by the fresh tracks on the path beneath my feet. Another set of human feet encased in diamond-soled Vasque boots had also recently trod the trail. No, I haven't made a study of the sole-impressions left by high-quality hiking boots. Those that preceded mine down the trail just happened to be new enough that the Vasque insignia left a clear impression in the space between toe and heel, a fact I noticed only after nudging aside some bear scat with the toe of my own hikers and discovering the trademark underneath. I didn't linger over the boot impression. All in all, judging the freshness of the scat seemed a lot more important at that moment than figuring out who those boots belonged to.

At the viewing site the boots of hundreds of permit-holding tourists had worn away the grass, leaving a barren circle of rocky soil fenced by thriving sedges about a foot high. A dozen or more trails passed nearby, some intersecting, others running parallel. All empty. I dropped my backpack and started to take a breath of relief. That's when a huge grizzly rambled out of the poplar a hundred feet upriver. I froze, unable to complete my inhalation, unable to sing, unable to do anything but watch helplessly as the bear came toward me, following a path leading straight to the viewing area.

A male, by the size of him, with a scruffy rust-colored coat that bore the scars of many healed wounds. He moved with an easy lope, massive paws swinging forward with pigeon-toed grace, huge fore-shoulders pumping on either side of the hump crowning his back. His massive head swung side to side, topped impossibly by cute, fuzzy teddy bear ears.

I swallowed convulsively, forcing down a bubble of hysteria. But it broke free, pouring into my mind with the lyric of one of Jessie's favorite Raffi tunes, all about teddy bear hugs.

Desperate to escape that absurd chorus, I took a step backward. Then another.

The grizzly stopped abruptly and stood there, head swinging from side to side. My heart kicked into a faster beat. I remembered the animal's poor eyesight and slowly raised and lowered my arms, hoping the red sleeves of my anorak would catch his attention. Then remembering Belle's advice to avoid looking a bear in the eye, I forced mine to look down and away. The corner of my backpack snagged the edge of my vision. No comfort to be found in a loaded gun just beyond reach.

Fight or flight? His choice, not mine. In speed, strength, and stamina, I was hopelessly outclassed. Not a serious tree in sight. I might reach the backpack. How about the gun? Maybe. Possibly. How possibly?

Impossibly. No chance. Never happen. Not before those four-inch claws reached me. Long after those incisors ripped flesh. Like Roland. Bloody bits. Shreds.

A shudder caught me then, and I squeezed my eyes tightly shut, steeling myself against the nightmare, willing the memory away. Time passed. Seconds? Minutes? Does it matter? When I opened my eyes again, the grizzly was gone. *That* mattered.

Gone but not far. He'd ambled along the trail and turned off on another that led down to the riverbank where he now stood, peering into the clear rush of water. Far enough! A sudden weakness swept me, and I sank down onto the barren soil of the viewing site, marveling at the invisible security fence afforded me by decades of peaceful coexistence between bears and man at McNeil River.

For the next hour or so I sat watching the bear. My bear now and named Teddy, of course. For about ten minutes he paced up and down the bank, stopping every few feet to nudge his snout toward the water in search of salmon. As Teddy searched, my heart gradually slowed to a normal resting beat. As a scientist, I hate having to confess to holding fuzzy-wuzzy feelings about any animal outside of family pets, but Teddy was special. Not in the sense of *New Age Naturalist*, you understand. In my confrontation with Teddy, bear and woman didn't "share" anything or "build a bridge" between species. What happened was actually pretty one-sided. I stood my ground. When a big old Alaskan brown bear came into view, I stood my ground. Victory!

After checking his favorite fishing holes, Teddy

found a hollow in the bank and flopped down for a snooze. Talk about trust! Until then I'd never really believed Roland's theories about a bear's intelligence and ability to learn. I'd dismissed stories about similar incidents at McNeil as exaggeration or just plain tall tales. Teddy's very survival depended on trusting his instincts, and those instincts had adapted to the presence of humans in the viewing area. He'd *learned* that those humans posed no threat. Suddenly it seemed monumentally important that Kirby Rogers not be allowed to teach Teddy a very different lesson about the humans at McNeil.

I scouted the immediate vicinity from the safety of the viewing site and found a spot that looked likely. The tangle of alder thicket behind me was at least a dozen yards from the nearest trail. After carefully eyeing the sleeping bear, I shouldered my pack and headed uphill. On closer inspection, the spot showed no sign of tracks or disturbed foliage, meaning—I hoped—that the bears steered clear for whatever reason. A glance at the limitless vista of river and sky, mountain and sea, suggested why. No species except man could use up every inch of the great land.

Setting up camp was as simple as shaking out my narrow two-man tent, staking the four corners and tying three rooflines to handy poplar. There was just enough room under the lowest branches to squeeze it in, which proved fortunate because the place was bug heaven. After dousing heavily with industrial-strength insect repellant, I hung my temple bell from a roofline and set up the video equipment, sharpening the lens focus on the sleeping bear a hundred yards below. A quick dart beyond the poplar proved my little camp invisible behind a rampart of green. After scooting inside the tent and zipping down, I dug a vacuum-sealed backpacker's zucchini lasagne out and ate it cold.

Outside the evening slowly faded to dusk, and shadows crept across the tent. For the first time I considered the possibility that Teddy's nonchalance was the result of senility rather than learning. Either way Kirby wasn't going to take my bear and get away with it. Every minute or so, I tapped the top right corner of my tent just hard enough to make the temple bell ring. I braved the clouds of insects outside only once, just long enough to crawl a dozen yards deeper into the poplar, scoop a shallow hole with my knife and bury my dinner's wrappings. For my trouble, I earned a zillion bites on my face and the peace of mind that comes with knowing that no scent of food emanated from my backpack or tent.

So the long night of brief darkness passed. Maybe I dozed but not for long. Fuzzy-wuzzy feelings or no, I wanted all bears forewarned of my presence and kept ringing my bell. Staying awake all night in June isn't hard in Alaska. Getting to sleep is. As the solstice nears, our twilights grow so long as to eliminate true night darkness. At least it feels that way. Up north of the Arctic Circle the sun rises in mid-May and doesn't set again until early August. For the rest of Alaska the sun does set but doesn't dip low enough under the horizon to cast true darkness. The atmosphere refracting the sun's rays bends light over the horizon. Plus in the great land the airglow—light emission caused by chemical reactions in the upper atmosphere—is particularly bright. All of which goes to explain why I was awake and relatively alert as the dim tide turned and day slowly began to brighten.

After gobbling breakfast of backpacker's honey-sweetened strawberry granola and burying the evidence, I took up my position behind the camera, ear cocked for the sound of Kirby Rogers's rotors. Leaving at dawn meant he'd be a good hour at least. If he got off on time.

The riverbank below me lay empty until twilight passed and true morning began. Birds twittered in the poplar around me, a warbling chorus welcoming the dawn. When the first bright rays streaked up behind the peaks to the east, painting crimson across purple clouds, a bear appeared on the farthest trail from my vantage point. I swung the camera and captured him in my viewfinder, recognizing Teddy's loping gait even before I focused in.

So did somebody else, somebody nearby, but I didn't know that yet. I didn't know that another human lurked in the poplar. I didn't know that his eye sighted down a telescopic scope or that his finger tightened on a high performance trigger. Not yet.

A rifleshot ripped through birdsong like a thunderclap, sending a winged multitude skyward. Below me, Teddy faltered, shaking his massive head.

I started forward blindly as the second shot came, the report soaring above the lingering echo of the first. That shot hit Teddy square on the skull and high, releasing a fountain of blood.

That's when I knew. And that's when I screamed.

18

Nnnn-ooooooo!"

I burst from the poplars and pivoted right, heading toward the source of the gunfire. The bear was still alive, still moving, wobbling slowly forward on a lopsided path aimed for the river. I couldn't see the gunman but knew for certain his finger still twitched on that trigger.

My boots slid on the dew-slicked grass, and I went down, pulled by gravity into a sideways tumble, barking knees and elbows and nose on rocks hidden under the lush grass. From somewhere up and behind me, a shout—words unintelligible. And then another rifle shot.

My long slide ended against a large rock that caught my middle. Inertia wrapped me around it with such force that my fingers actually touched the toes of my boots. When I could lift my head, I looked for the bear. He lay sprawled on the riverbank near the bottom of the falls, a seep of blood from his wrecked skull draining into the white rush of hissing water. I lowered my head to the damp grass, and a moan escaped me, inspired by equal parts of pain, frustration, and despair. So much for Lauren Maxwell, defender of the wild.

The roar of the falls cloaked the gunman's emergence from his hiding place in the poplars with a shield of thunder. I heard nothing—not the rustle of leaves on whip-sawing branches, not the clinking ejection of a spent shell, not the squeaking tramp of heavily shod feet. Without warning, his muddy, almost-new Vasques appeared within my narrow field of vision. And, before I could react, passed on.

As the distance between us increased, he gradually grew. The pair of booted feet proved the ends of blue-jeaned legs. Now into sight rose a narrow back carrying a Pendleton plaid and an L.L. Bean backpack. Last of all, I saw his head, cropped salt-and-pepper hair topped with a visored cap. He stopped a dozen feet from the bear, rammed home a cartridge and fired another round into that shattered skull.

For one wild second I imagined him turning around, chambering another cartridge, and finishing me off as well. And yet for all that, I sensed no menace in him, no threat that put me on my guard. Part of me expected him to move on to the grizzly and examine his kill, prodding the trophy with his foot and weighing a clawed paw in his hand. When he didn't, when he turned and started back in my direction, I felt no surprise. And no apprehension.

I struggled free of the rock and managed to get to my knees by the time he reached me. We'd had a chance to study each other as he approached. I'd noted the solemn brown eyes above the full bush beard. He'd noted the bloody scrapes on my cheek and nose.

He stopped in front of me. "I got some stuff for those cuts." He shouldered the rifle with one hand and offered me the other. "Come on."

Outrage provided the burst of energy I needed to get to my feet. I swatted his hand aside and rose from the crushed grass. "Who the hell are you? And what the fuck do you think you're doing killing that grizzly? This is a game sanctuary."

He started to answer, but something stayed his words, something behind me that also caught his eye. I turned, expecting another grizzly but saw nothing.

The gunman raised a hand, pointing north and east. "There. A chopper."

A dark speck against the pinking dawn, the helicopter grew just as the gunman had, silhouette taking shape as it flew closer, but rotors unheard beneath the torrent of the falls. The backlighting that made spotting the helicopter easy also threw the interior in shadow. The pilot remained invisible. But I didn't have to actually see Kirby Rogers to know he was flying that chopper. Or to realize he wouldn't be stealing any bears for my camera that day.

"God damn it to hell." I spun back to the gun-toting stranger who'd killed my bear and spoiled my trap. The rifleman still watched the approaching helicopter, one hand raised to shade his eyes against the rising sun. "God damn you, too, pal. You sure fucked everything up royally."

In a sudden blur of motion his free arm swung up and I was down again. The stranger landed on my back and pinned my neck with an iron hand, pressing my face into the grass. I struggled for only an instant.

When the *CRACK-CRACK* of rifle shots finally penetrated my anger and surprise, I lay still. Kirby Rogers was helo-hunting again, and this time his quarry was human.

As the helicopter closed, spewing sparks of death from a gun mounted on one skid, the stranger counterattacked, elbowing into firing position and squeezing off two rounds. Then he wrapped an arm around me and started rolling across the hillside, presenting a moving target to the maniac hovering above.

The helicopter rose suddenly, and the stranger grabbed the opportunity. Lacing a hand through the leather belt at the back of my waist, he lifted me from the ground and hauled me up the hill.

I chanced a look back. The chopper had swung up and around. Now a zipper of rifle shots chased us, tossing up chunks of grass and soil. I dived for the poplars.

CRACK-CRACK-CRACK.

The stranger followed me in, exhaling a rush of panting words. "Sixteen, seventeen, eighteen." He laid a hand on the calf of my outstretched leg and squeezed. "Keep going. He's not out of ammo yet."

I bellied forward, angling to the right for a thick fence of saplings, fear bittering my mouth. My God, Kirby *had* killed Roland! And he was ready to kill again.

CRACK.

The shot clipped through the poplars overhead, shearing off twigs and leaves. I tossed a look back at the stranger. "Nineteen."

He wormed up beside me. "I'm betting his limit's twenty."

We lay still for long minutes but never did find out. The rumble of the falls carried up the hill and into the copse of poplars, drowning the roar of rotors. I rested my head on crossed arms and closed my eyes, too tired and too scared to think, let alone move. An insect buzzed somewhere nearby, and the sun rose high enough to send slanting rays through the thick canopy of leaves overhead. The stranger clocked a final five minutes on his wristwatch and crawled off to check on Kirby.

Sometime later he hailed me through the screen of saplings and announced it safe to come out. Safe? With him around? On aching hands and bruised knees, I made my way out into the sunshine. As awareness of my wounds resurfaced, so did my anger. Not only had the stranger killed a bear, he'd almost gotten me killed as well. That may sound like ingratitude, but I'd roller-coastered through too much to be reasonable right then. Anger—a strong, empowering emotion—won out.

Again the stranger offered me his hand. Again I swatted it aside. His eyes widened with surprise, and he took a step back, dropping his hand. I came after him step for step, raising a verbal storm around his ears.

"The man piloting that helicopter is a criminal. He's been taking bears and airlifting them over the border to private hunts for fat cats. A good friend of mine wanted to expose him and died trying." The memory of Roland injected a stutter into my voice. "N-n-n-now he's s-s-s-slipped free again. Thanks to y-y-you."

I walked away from the stranger, taking deep calming breaths. But when I regained my composure, I was after him once more. In the few minutes that took, he hadn't moved. Or spoken.

"Not that you give a shit. After all, why should you? You've obviously got no respect for this place or these animals. No matter where you find them, grizzlies are strictly for killing." I smirked up at him. "Isn't that right?"

"As a matter of fact, it is."

Surprise had fled his dark brown eyes long since and been replaced with a weary resignation that failed to match the challenge of his words. Confusion left me speechless for a second. Poachers seldom confess, even when caught red-handed. But in the end my underlying anger managed to boil up more words. And burn away the last of my common sense.

"That's great. Just great. So how long have you been on this private hunt of yours? How many bears have you killed? And how long are you planning to stay?"

He looked past me, scanning the horizon where he first spotted the helicopter. "I'm on sixty days' leave. Killed fourteen bears so far and got two weeks left." His eyes dropped to meet mine. "Looked to me like those criminals of yours wore uniforms. Flying government aircraft, too. Think they'll be back?"

The realization of my utter vulnerability returned at that moment and robbed me of speech. Not that the stranger had threatened me. On the contrary, he'd actually started out by offering me first aid. And when Kirby began shooting, the stranger had shielded my body with his own. And I'd turned on him with a snarl. *TWICE!* Twice I'd faced him off like a rabid dog. Now I was at his mercy. Literally. He had the rifle and, obviously, the will to use it. And with fourteen dead bears to his credit, plenty of reason, too. Behind his question lay something unspoken, but what exactly? I decided to take the initiative by asking. "Are you going to kill me next?"

I stood my ground as he studied me, his solemn brown eyes taking in the thrust of my chin, straight back, and clenched fists, acknowledging my refusal to drop my eyes or my bravado. Finally he shook his head and cracked a small smile. "Nnnaahh. What I'm going to do is take you upriver a ways. Show you where those criminals of yours get their bears."

With that, the stranger turned and headed at a good lope for an upstream trail, casually slinging the rifle over one shoulder.

I stumbled after him. "But why?"

He tossed an explanation over one shoulder without slackening speed. "Because you remind me of Jen. My daughter."

More than once that afternoon I entertained second thoughts about my safety and my sanity. Maybe the stranger was simply luring me deeper into the wild, the better to hide my murdered body. On the one hand, the possibility seemed perfectly plausible. On the other hand, I didn't believe that for an instant. I sensed no threat in the man, only a curious sorrow. Which was what made me doubt my sanity. Look where my senses had led me thus far.

Our travels reprised the bushwhacking I'd done with Belle. Like my Athabascan friend, the stranger stopped often, pausing to listen for grizzlies. That's when we exchanged information about who and why. His name turned out to be Aaron Whittier. He CPOed on a Trident nuclear sub that sometimes stayed down for weeks, which explained his ability to perform under pressure. Hah-hah. I didn't ask why he was killing bears and he didn't say. Not yet.

"You must have great eyesight. I couldn't even make out the people through that shadow." I gently fingered a particularly painful bruise on my elbow and wondered how much further my battered body could go. "And uniforms—forget it."

He grinned down at me. "Neither could I. I saw the uniforms when they got themselves a bear a few weeks ago."

My head snapped up. "You saw them take a bear? Where?"

He nodded down the trail. "Further on a piece."

"A piece" turned out to be about two more miles, but I didn't complain once Aaron Whittier had shown me the culvert trap hidden in the scrub. Kirby Rogers had airlifted in the essential tool for grizzly grabbing—a bear-proof trap. Usually the metal cylinders are mounted on a trailer, but this trap was stripped down for flying and lay directly on the ground. The drop door in front and rear trigger were strictly standard. So was the timer that released the door when humans were safely away and the bacon used as bait.

"When I saw the way those brownies go for bacon, I wished I'd brought more myself." Aaron Whittier shook his head at the memory. "Imagine me coming on it sudden, the bear already in the trap and not a soul to be seen. I had my killshot sighted before I got to thinking."

I kept my eyes steady on the culvert trap. "You were going to kill a trapped bear?"

"You bet. Then I got to wondering what was up and found myself a nice hidey-hole in the brush." He pointed out the place. "Next day two choppers come in. One's government issue with two uniforms inside —man and woman. They got here first and put the bear to sleep. Then comes the other man, flying solo with no markings. He took the bear."

So Kirby Rogers had an accomplice. A female accomplice. That figured. All fair in love and war for *Scumbag americanus*. Apparently, the same philosophy guided Aaron Whittier. And yet he didn't strike me as a Kirby Rogers kind of man.

"Those three I can understand. They want the money. But you I don't understand." I turned to him then and raised my eyes to meet his. "You're just killing. Wantonly. For no reason."

"That's where you're wrong. I have reason." His eyes flashed fire, scaring me for the first time. "Wound for wound, stripe for stripe, life for life. A grizzly ate my girl, Jen. That's reason to kill 'em all."

19

Aaron Whittier's horrifying revelation was the last word spoken between us for many miles. What could I say? The ubiquitous *I'm sorry* had never seemed more inadequate. *Sorry* just did not cut it for a man whose daughter had been eaten by a bear. No one knew that better than I. After all, I'd lost my friend Roland Taft to the bears. And my husband, Max, to the wild.

Right after he dropped that bombshell, Aaron Whittier headed back toward the coast, moving silently away from the culvert trap. I trailed after him, respecting his space by maintaining a five-foot interval. His need to avenge Jen's death didn't surprise me. Hadn't a surge of satisfaction swept me when I learned that the bear which killed Roland was dead? But Aaron Whittier had moved beyond vengeance into the realm of the seriously crazy, and his madness had to stop. No question about that. In fact, the only question was whether I could stop him on my own, without the assistance of the law.

My steps dragged. Afternoon was well launched, and I hadn't eaten since breakfast. I dug through my pockets and, finding nothing edible, cursed the recklessness of leaving my daypack back at camp. Who cared that the cinnamon granola bar tucked inside had been there long enough to be staled twice over? Surely not my growling stomach. At the next spring that trickled across the trail, I knelt and filled my Sierra cup, hoping to slake both hunger and thirst. That didn't work for long. A few minutes later I put aside the niceties of mourning and broke into a trot to catch up with Aaron Whittier. Then I shamelessly begged for food.

His smile didn't reach eyes freed now of fury and sorrowing once again. He handed me his rifle and swung the Bean pack from his back. The unexpected weight of the weapon in my hands was alien and unwelcome. I wanted to be rid of it. Adding to my discomfort was my continuing obligation to Aaron Whittier. The lifesaving generosity of the bush is legendary, but being asked sure beats begging.

After he'd rummaged a while in his pack, I traded the gun for an orange and a package of peanut butter and crackers. We sat down right there on an open hillside that sloped gently toward the river and ate our meal in the rare sunshine of southwest Alaska. I noted with approval how he tossed the orange peel and cracker package back into his pack. At least he wasn't a slob hunter.

He finished his food and stretched out on the thick grass, wedging the knapsack under his head and tilting his cap to shade his eyes from the glare. I stared down at the river, squinting against the sun-dazzled brilliance, and gathered my courage to ask the question that had been dogging me for miles. "Tell me about Jen."

My words hung in the air, unanswered so long his voice startled me when he finally spoke. "Until a year ago I had three goals in life. Seeing my baby girl happy was Number One."

He lay still, face hidden by his cap. Except for his lips, now trembling, now firm. "The others were finishing out a thirty-year stretch in the navy and homesteading a piece of Yukon riverfront we staked out fifteen years ago. She was just a bitty thing then."

His lips twisted. "My ex didn't like me bringing our little girl up here." And twitched. "Maybe she was right."

For a few moments he lay silent and still. Then he sighed heavily and resumed his story. "But what could she do? After she traded me in for a man with a career on shore, she had a couple more kids. All I had left was Jen. I spent every leave with that girl. Every bit of it."

Suddenly he snatched the cap from his face and rolled onto his side, pinning me in place with a stare. "She was something. Smart and pretty and strong. And she loved this country. Came up here for college in the end. Spent her time roaming the back country."

His eyes went distant and dreamy. "She wanted to work in the bush. Took a degree in science. 'Can you believe it, Daddy? Getting paid for work that's so much fun?' Loved it. She said exactly that last time we talked. She just loved her life so much.

"She got a job down in Katmai Park." He fell back against the knapsack and closed his eyes. "Counting birds to see how many drowned in the *Exxon Valdez* slick."

His face twisted into a mask of anguish. "A grizzly came into camp and dragged her out of her tent. My beautiful Jen. My baby girl."

I turned away and buried my face in my shoulder, feeling like a voyeur for watching as long as I had. Honest grief is the most terrifying sight on earth because it is death made visible, living and breathing death. And down deep each of us knows that grief is waiting for us. I knew better than most.

Sometime later, Aaron Whittier rose from the ground and started down the trail. Again without a word. And again I stumbled after him, five-foot interval intact, as much for my benefit now as his. I was not yet ready to pay for his story with one of my own. Later, maybe. But not yet.

The sun had started to sink by the time we approached the falls. Too late to light a signal fire on the beach. The TNC helicopter pilot surely had flown his last load to Iliamna by now. The idea of spending another night on the heights above McNeil Falls did not excite me, not with a grizzly lying dead below. I hoped Aaron Whittier would help move my camp down to the beach and then stay for supper. That would give me a chance to try to end his slaughter.

He heard the bears before I did and stopped, lifting a warning hand. I froze and tried to peer through the screen of poplars. A low, throaty growl drifted on the breeze. My heart clenched. A deep, bellowing roar rose above the thunder of the falls. I scurried toward the safety of Aaron Whittier's rifle. "What is going on?"

He shrugged. "Sounds like a couple of bears found the brownie I killed and are having it out." He checked his rifle for ammunition. "Stay close."

I stuck so close the toes of my boots touched the heels of his. I'd thought nothing could equal my fear when charged by the grizzly sow. But sound must surpass sight on the fright meter because the hair on my arms and neck stiffened painfully as we crept toward the source of the roaring. My heart kicked into a gallop. And I had to consciously slow my breathing to keep from hyperventilating. I was *that* scared.

Part of which came from standing out in the open—in plain view!—as two half-ton grizzlies fought it out over the carcass of a third. Aaron Whittier hissed an answer to my panicked question. "Damn straight they'll see us. That's what we want. Never leave a grizzly guessing about what's rustling the bushes." He shook his head. "Jesus, you should know that."

A hundred yards below, the bears ignored us. One was a silvertip sow with a cub in tow. Her bloody-muzzled offspring cowered behind the now-gaping haunch of my bear. Junior's presence provided Mama with an added incentive for guarding their dinner at any cost. She looked to have the upper hand in the encounter. Her roars and aggressive stance had succeeded in halting the approach of an adolescent male who had planned to share the feast. Poor fellow had misjudged badly and was now in very deep. He'd assumed the textbook challenge posture—ears back, hindquarters crouched, head down, mouth opened for a low, continuous growl. Extricating himself from the confrontation might be tough. Any sign of appeasement could prompt the sow to attack.

The play-by-play analysis calmed me and allowed my rational scientific side to reassert itself. As the confrontation progressed, Aaron Whittier and I watched without fear, mesmerized by a drama as old as nature. Thanks to Charles Darwin, we were able to follow the script.

Survival of the fittest is a notion with many layers of meaning. On the most basic level, the carcass of my bear was an unbelievable treasure for both contending grizzlies—a caloric mother lode just waiting to be eaten, gained without expending an ounce of the precious energy reserves needed to survive the next winter. Junior's existence added extra dimensions of significance for the sow. His survival expressed her fitness as a mother. In addition, his continued existence doubled the chances of her genetic survival. In other words, winning *really* counted for the sow.

Aaron Whittier agreed. "Plus she's got him beat on size. By two hundred pounds, at least."

Without warning, the sow charged, ears flattened and bared teeth gnashing over a throaty growl. The young male reacted quickly, rising up on hind legs to appear larger and show his readiness to fight. The sow pulled up and stopped just short of bowling into him. She let loose a final roar and then backed off a few steps. The male dropped to the ground and just stood there, still snapping his mouth but no longer growling. The sow slowly moved back toward her cub, never quite turning her back on the male or taking her eyes off him. He started edging back as well, all the while silently snapping his teeth.

I turned to Aaron Whittier and found him sighting the male down the barrel of his rifle. Without thinking, I reached out and grabbed the gun, inserting my hand into his line of sight. "Don't." He stiffened. "Please don't."

He lowered the rifle and shrugged, not meeting my

eyes. I touched his arm. "Would you give me a hand moving my stuff to the beach? The offer includes dinner."

The extra food I'd packed came in handy that night. When the water on the Primus stove reached a steady boil, I gave Aaron Whittier first choice of the half dozen dinners I'd brought. He choose three: beef bourguignonne, Cantonese shrimp, and chicken paprikash. I settled on turkey asparagus and plopped all four foil envelopes into the water to heat through.

We'd made camp in the area used by tourists with permits who visit McNeil each summer. That's where the bears expected us to be. I'd left my tent in its sack and spread my sleeping bag on a cropped tarp. My dinner guest pulled a grimy down bag from his pack, along with a variety of first-aid supplies, which he insisted on dabbing, blotting, and bandaging over my face once I'd taken care of my arms and legs.

After gently smoothing a Band-Aid over a scrape beneath my right eye, he sat back and slowly shook his head. "There's nothing I can do about that shiner of yours."

I fingered the puffy flesh, surprisingly the only area of my body that didn't ache unmercifully. "My kids will absolutely howl when they see it. Then they'll dash for the cameras."

He busied himself repacking his first-aid kit. "What about your husband? I'll bet he won't be pleased."

I waited until he finished with his bandages, wanting his undivided attention. When the zipper of his pack closed over his gear, I launched my first salvo.

"My husband is dead." I pointed over his left shoulder, vaguely north by northwest. "He's out there somewhere. Maybe the Kilbuck Mountains. Maybe the Kuskokwim Delta. I didn't know then, and I don't know now. Probably never will."

Using tongs and a pocketknife, I grabbed a foil dinner from the boiling water and sliced it open. Beef bourguignonne. One of his. After handing over his first course, I fished out my own dinner and pretended to eat. Mostly my mouthfuls were for effect, pauses to add punctuation to my tale.

"Max wanted Alaska, not me. I would have been happy to settle in some out-of-the-way place in the Lower Forty-eight. Oregon, say. Maybe Idaho. Or Montana." I spooned up a piece of asparagus and ate it slowly. Bland. I'd bought it for a family trip, one when Jessie'd been in a finicky stage. "None of those places would have worked for Max. He wanted something more. Needed something more. At first I fought him, but in the end I recognized his need."

My guest was ready for more. I spooned out the Cantonese shrimp. The aroma left me wondering if the turkey asparagus had been a mistake.

"Max needed the wild. Wild places and wild things. He needed challenge and danger. And sometimes he needed to test the edge. Without the edge, part of him just dulled up and died." Another spoonful brought a chunk of turkey. Better than mushy asparagus but just barely. "So we came to Alaska. And coming here brought him back to life. He loved it. He just loved his life so much."

Aaron Whittier looked at me then and nodded, acknowledging my use of his very words about Jen to tell my own story of loss. I looked away, letting my eyes sweep full circle over the waves on Kamishak Bay and the cinder cone of Augustine Island, to climb the serrated ridges of the Aleutian Range at his back and to roam the endless tundra at mine.

Turning back, I flung my arms wide. "This is what Max wanted, what he loved. I can't hate it for taking him away from me. He loved his life so much. And risk was part of it. A big part."

Aaron Whittier turned down his third course of chicken paprikash. The weight of my words and my wounds had killed my appetite as well. We bundled up the remnants of our meals and buried our garbage. He asked how I planned to get home, and I told him about my arrangement with the TNC helicopter pilot. He nodded and spoke the words that made all my aches seem worthwhile. "Think I can hitch a ride?"

20

As predicted, my kids took one look at my black eye and really whooped it up for a couple of minutes. Then they raced for my closet, in search of cameras. I can't be the only Mom who records her children's every bruise, break, and stitch for posterity. Childhood immunizations have eliminated diseases like measles, mumps, and rubella as threats to survival for those children whose families can afford the shots. So what other chances do kids have for esteem-building, for overcoming and triumphing? Jessie still "wows" over the close-up I snapped of the jagged edge of the front tooth she chipped as a toddler. That was one the Tooth Fairy didn't get. And Jake still winces at the gory shot of the thumb he sliced when he mistook it for a whittling stick. The scar may have faded long ago, but he still has the photograph to impress his friends. And plenty of others that are proof that pain does indeed fade in time and bad things truly can be overcome.

The most that can be said of my session in front of the cameras is that I endured it. The kids danced before me, firing off one flash-shot on each of the cameras. How did we wind up with so many? The fact that both of them had a pal over didn't help. When Jessie's friend saw that shiner, she plugged a thumb into her mouth, and the sight inspired a *Wait-till-they-hear-this* gloat on the face of Jake's buddy. Nina poked her head out of the kitchen long enough to cluck in sympathy but quickly returned to serving up the chili when she concluded I'd live. Turned out the whole gang had tickets for a Glacier Pilots game at Mulcahy Park and planned to eat and run. Travis MacDonald, the organizer of the outing, explained that as he shooed the tribe of youngsters back into the family room to eat their dinner off TV trays.

"Great. Have a good time." I thought about grabbing my pack again but decided to leave it where it'd fallen when the clan swarmed out to greet me. "I'll be in the shower."

Nina popped out of the kitchen again. "But I've got your dinner on the table." She grinned. "Along with a very cold beer."

I hesitated. "Did you ice the glass?"

Her nod decided it. Hot chili and cold beer just might be the tonic I needed to see me through the evening. After the two-day fiasco at the game sanctuary, I had plenty of thinking to do and lots of decisions to make. Before eating, I ducked into the powder room to wash up and run a comb through my hair. And to review the carefully edited version of events I'd concocted on the long drive from Homer. Simply telling the truth was out of the question. A maniac helo-hunting for humans? A grieving father bent on exterminating the grizzly? Hearing the truth might prompt Nina and Travis to do something outrageous like try to stop me from going back. And I *was* going back. That decision had already been made.

Travis allowed me three mouthfuls of chili and one sip of beer before demanding an explanation for my battered appearance. "I've seen prizefighters come out of the ring looking a lot better, Lauren. No offense. But what the hell happened?"

Across the table Nina's eyes begged for an answer as well. I laid aside my spoon, fortified myself with a gulp of beer, and then began spinning my deceitful little web. "I slipped and fell. Can you believe it? And the way I look isn't the worst of it. Not by a longshot." I paused and looked from one to the other, good friends both who had to be misled. Then I blinked my eyes and forced a catch into my voice. "The worst of it is that I wound up scaring Kirby Rogers away. In other words, I blew it. I completely blew it."

A mean strategy, but it worked. True friends want you to succeed. They root for you and cheer you on. When you fail, a true friend succors your wounds and hears out your woe. And invariably offers the same bit of advice: *Don't dwell on it.* Those friends with tact take their own advice and quickly let you off the hook by dropping the subject. The furtive glance Travis and Nina exchanged promised that tact would soon triumph over curiosity.

Travis crushed a saltine and let the crumbs fall into his chili. "I'd like to hear about it. That is—"

"—that is, if you feel like talking. Right, Trav?" Nina flashed a pasted-on smile at him. "If you don't want to talk about it yet, we'll understand."

"Weellll." I sniffed hard and then let out a deep

sigh. "At dawn I was all set up and just waiting for Kirby to show up. Pretty soon I could see him coming, a little dark speck on the horizon which grew larger as he got closer. I checked my camera again, got it in focus. And the next thing I know there's this guy at the viewing site above the falls. I mean, here comes Kirby Rogers to grab his grizzly, and there is a guy just standing there."

That caught their interest. Mysteries always do. Nina wanted to know who he was. Travis wanted to know where he came from. I just shrugged impatiently and went on with the story.

"I yelled but he couldn't hear me over the falls. So I decided to run out there and make him get out of sight. Which is when I fell. I mean, I really fell." I raised scabbed elbows to illustrate the point. "Face first and then *bing-bang-boom* off all these rocks hidden in the grass. A volcanic formation, so they were sharp."

Nina got her question in first. "The man heard you and helped, didn't he?"

"Oh, yeah." I touched the Band-Aid under my eye. "I was a little dazed, as you'd imagine. He came running and whipped out his first-aid kit. Turns out he's in the navy and had some medical training. He insisted on checking me for broken bones. I'm trying to get up and get us both under cover, and he's running his hands up and down my legs. And here comes goddamned Kirby Rogers in his helicopter for a bird's-eye view. But he sure didn't stay long."

"Imagine what that looked like." Travis threw me a wicked grin. "Proximity to danger rates high as an aphrodisiac, I hear. If bears really are attracted to the scent, then that goes double. From what you've said about this guy, I'll bet he thought you were planning a little outdoor sport-fucking."

Nina loosed a bark of laughter, and I forced a cackle of my own. I had to admit the idea was pretty funny. If only it had really happened that way. Then I might be able to face the prospect of returning to the McNeil River game sanctuary with a bit of *sangfroid*. As it was, my determination to go back inspired a deep sense of gloom and forboding. Kirby Rogers had reacted to my presence at McNeil by opening fire. I'd tipped my hand to him by defending Roland's sanity when he chased me down that corridor at ADF&G. To Kirby, I now represented a threat that had to be eliminated. My survival depended on nailing him first. Which meant I had to go back to McNeil and film a bear theft, or I'd have no evidence to prove my allegations. My only comfort was the certainty that Kirby Rogers would never expect me to return to McNeil River. To be honest, though, if I was that certain, then how come I also felt as if I might be making the biggest mistake of my life?

I raised a toasting glass toward Travis and smiled. "Tell me that you, at least, got your baddy."

He shook his head. "I wish I could. We do have a better fix on the pilot, though."

Jake walked into the kitchen in time to hear that and started to fill in the blanks. "Yeah. Definitely a woman, and she's lousy on the stick of a helicopter, too."

The alarm on his wristwatch started to beep, and he threw up his arms. "You guys! Come on! We'll be late for the game."

Everybody scrambled at once—Jake to rouse the other kids, Nina to clear the table, and Travis to fire up the engine of his rig. Jessie zoomed out of the family room and into my arms, planting a string of sweet kisses across my bruised cheeks. "You take a nice bath and then go to bed, Mama. And you'll feel better in the morning." I kissed her back and waved a hand to answer the goodbye Jake tossed over his shoulder. Nina paused long enough to apologize for the sink full of dirty dishes and urge me to leave them before she, too, was gone.

I took Jessie's advice and ran a bath. The throbbing of my many wounds made it easy to take up Nina's offer to skip KP that night. A sudden spurt of resentment at being left home alone added extra incentive. Max would have understood how I was feeling. In some ways, the changed role in life that his death thrust upon me had helped me understand him better. There were times when he'd resented me and our children, times when we ran out of the house to some activity that excluded him and left him wondering if breadwinner was the only role his family wanted him to play in their lives. The flip side of that was including him in all our plans, which proved to be just as cruel because the unpredictability of his schedule so often forced him to "miss" long-planned activities. Now I found myself stuck in the same rut and feeling just as surly. Last week I'd warned both Nina and Travis that I might have to leave for the game sanctuary on very short notice. Still, being asked to the baseball game would have been nice.

My nice, long jasmine-scented bath didn't last long enough to wash me free of self-pity. Beyond my bathroom door, the phone rang and I let it. For Jessie or Jake or Nina, no doubt. I'd worked hard for the dollars that bought the answering machine that my children and housemate now took for granted. Just like they took a lot of other things for granted. Me, for instance. I settled myself chin deep in the tub and let that telephone wail.

I don't make a habit of feeling sorry for myself, but there are times when all of us wallow in misery. Surely I deserved my wallow that night. In the past six weeks I'd been through hell. I'd had a good friend eaten by a bear and slogged through miles of bush to discover that his death was no accident. I'd bawled at the charge of my first grizzly and stood fast in the presence of my second. I'd nose-dived across a rock-strewn meadow in a futile attempt to save Teddy and bellyflopped through an alder thicket in a successful attempt to save myself. I'd slogged through more miles of bush to discover the site of the grizzly grabs and managed to soothe the grief of a raving father. And like so many martyrs, I'd emerged from my crucible of terror and triumph with a tale that couldn't be told. Not yet, at least.

Imagine my irritation when I emerged from the tub and discovered the answering machine switched off. Those calls might have been for me! I'd salved the last of my scrapes and slipped into a soft and cuddly robe when the Trimline on my bedside table shrilled again. I snatched up the receiver and found Julianne Blanchard on the line.

"Mrs. Maxwell! I've been calling and calling!" Her breathless voice vibrated with excitement. "How did it go?"

"It didn't. It was a disaster." I eased onto my bed and burrowed my sore shoulders into a mound of pillows. This was one person I could tell the truth. She more than deserved that for all the risks she'd run.

"Just before Kirby arrived, this fellow turned up who started shooting the bears. Then in comes your boss with both barrels blazing."

Julianne squeaked. "He shot you?"

I let a sigh of satisfaction escape. Truth-telling can be such a relief. "No, he didn't shoot me. Or the other guy. He shot *at* us, actually. And with only one gun. The guy with me shot back, but I don't think he hit anything."

A long pause from Julianne and then she came back, even more tentative than usual. Honest questions came hard to her. She'd hidden her true feelings for too long to find exposure of any kind easy, even with someone she could trust. "I don't understand. You took somebody with you?"

"No. This guy just showed up. A man named Aaron Whittier. A grizzly killed his daughter down at Katmai Park last year, and he was out for vengeance. He hurt so bad he went a little crazy. He wanted to kill all the bears." I took a deep, slightly impatient breath. She didn't need to know this stuff. "Anyway, he's not important. He flew out with me, so he won't be killing any more bears."

Another squeak. "I see."

But I could tell she didn't understand and wished I'd never mentioned Aaron Whittier. I'd made a unilateral decision not to pursue legal action against him for the grizzly slaughter, and keeping my mouth shut would have made that easier. Now Julianne might press for prosecution. But if she did, I'd find a way to head her off. She might not understand and she didn't have to. All she had to do was let me know the next time the pattern of behaviors emerged that showed that Kirby Rogers was planning another grizzly grab. For once, she agreed without the usual hours of persuasion.

She squeaked like Minnie Mouse. "You can count on me."

"That's great, Julianne." I didn't bother to stifle the huge yawn that had been building all through our conversation. "I'll look forward to your call."

No way that last bit was the truth. Who in my position could honestly look forward to another round with either Kirby Rogers or the McNeil River bears? The first lie between Julianne Blanchard and Lauren Maxwell had been spoken. Or so I thought.

21

My recovery got off to a smooth start the next morning. I woke up slightly stiff but free of self-pitying funk and ready to immerse myself in the mothering and household chores I'd neglected lately. School was just out for the summer, leaving the kids in a holiday mood. Togetherness was the theme of the day. We poached our breakfast eggs together. We washed and waxed the 4-Runner together. We fixed the rock work on Esther the otter's pool together. And we'd just started weeding the garden together when the bell at the front door bonged, resounding through the empty house until the echo wafted through open windows to reach us out back.

Jake darted into the house to answer the door and returned minutes later with an announcement no mother wants to hear. "Mom, there's a policeman here to see you. A detective!"

Suddenly my recovery got very rocky very fast. I peered into the shadowed house at my son, squinting against the sun to judge whether those wide eyes meant he was joking. The nervous glance he shot over his shoulder and tremble of excitement in his voice persuaded me that he wasn't kidding. "Come on, Mom. He's waiting."

Suddenly another shadow appeared behind Jake, towering over my tall son. The cop opened the screen door and followed Jake onto the deck. I barely managed to brush the dirt from my hands when he was there in front of me, offering me a glimpse of a badge pinned in his wallet. "Matthew Shcridan, Anchorage police. Are you Lauren Maxwell?"

My effort to rise faltered when a cramp locked up my thigh. He reached down with both hands and cupped my elbows, lifting me to my feet. He held me a few seconds longer than necessary, long seconds he spent studying my bruised and bandaged face. When his hands dropped away, I took a step backward. "Thank you."

I smoothed my hair with jittery fingers. Cops make me feel guilty even when I have nothing to hide. Unfortunately, that day I was hiding plenty. "I'm Lauren Maxwell. What is this about?"

He tossed a quick glance at the wide eyes of both children and folded his arms. "If I could speak with you alone?"

Little bubbles of panic rose in my throat, and I fought to keep my voice even. The result came out too bright to be real. "Jake and Jessie—why don't you take five in the family room? See if there's anything good on the tube."

If possible, my children's bug eyes widened further. Never before had I admitted that there could sometimes be "good" programming on TV. And very seldom did I issue my children an open invitation to watch the damned thing. (Can't say never on that one. *All* of us use the electronic babysitter sometime.) But in spite of the rarity of this occurrence, both kids were tempted to stay. Visiting detectives arrived at our house even less frequently. Sensing the possibility that their reluctance could escalate into a scene, I sweetened the offer. "And while you're at it, have a Dove bar."

That sent them galloping inside. And lit a gleam of amusement in the Anchorage cop's blue eyes. "I can't believe Dove bars are that much better."

"Oh, they're not. But kids really believe what they hear on TV. At least mine do." I sank into a faded blue canvas director's chair and offered the other to him, feeling more at ease suddenly. Which was probably the whole point of his comment.

I straightened my back, wanting to regain control. "You said your name is Sheridan?" He nodded and I gave him my most gracious smile. Phony as hell. "Well, then, Detective Sheridan, what can I do for you?"

He took his time, giving me the opportunity to study him. The first thing I decided was that he didn't look much like a cop. The rumpled blue blazer, narrow knit tie, and pleated twill pants didn't fit. Out of uniform, cops preferred polyester. That's what Vanessa Larrabee always told me, and she'd dated half the municipal force. I was about to throw the impostor out when he settled the question with three neat moves.

First, he unbuttoned the sportcoat, allowing me a glimpse of the holster strapped under his arm. Second, he drew a plastic bag from an inner pocket and held it up so I could see the business card inside. *My* business card. Finally he asked the obvious question. "Is this your card?"

I nodded, convinced of his authenticity, and asked an obvious question of my own. "Where did you get it?"

Only real cops and good reporters ask such obvious questions. Neither breed minds looking dense when gathering information because both hate being wrong when it counts. For a cop that means on the witness stand, and for a reporter that means in print. Asking the obvious questions helps both to get it right.

Matthew Sheridan stuffed the bag back in his pocket and drew out a small notebook, flipping it open. "Do you know a man named Aaron Whittier?"

The name hit me like a punch. And it showed. I sagged against the chair. Damn Julianne Blanchard! She'd squealed and they'd caught him. And probably wanted me to testify. I sighed deeply. "I know him."

"He's a friend of yours?"

"Yes, sort of." My scientist's need for precision remained but not the ability to voice it. "But not really."

Sheridan cocked his head to one side and raised an eyebrow in my direction.

"I mean, I met him camping. Just the other day." I spread my arms. "Look, I started off asking what this is about. Maybe it's time you told me."

"Right." Sheridan laid his notebook on one long thigh and leveled serious eyes on me. "Mrs. Maxwell, I am investigating the death of Aaron Whittier."

I gasped. "Dead?" The news left me sputtering in search of understanding. "When? Where? How?"

The detective glanced at his notebook. "A motel

maid found him in his room late this morning. Just how he died is the subject of this investigation. Suicide is one possibility. Would that surprise you?"

That took about one second's thought. Aaron Whittier was not a happy man. "No."

Sheridan turned a page in his notebook and jotted a quick note. "So you knew him to be despondent."

I nodded, relieved now to be on solid ground. "Oh, yeah. He was pretty unhappy."

The detective raised his blue eyes, zeroing in to throw me the zinger. "For somebody who didn't know him long, you seem pretty well informed."

That succeeded in shutting me up. The world tilted into confusion. Suddenly nothing seemed certain. What exactly were we talking about here?

Before I could ask, Sheridan threw me a lifeline. "We need your help, Mrs. Maxwell." His smile brimmed with reassurance. "As far as we can tell, you're the only person in Anchorage who actually knew Aaron Whittier. We need you to identify the body."

I stiffened, instantly ready to refuse. Scientist or no—yeech! But he raised a hand. "Please, Mrs. Maxwell. There won't be anything gory about it. Sleeping pills. He just went to sleep and never woke up."

What a sucker! At least I fell for a classic. Generations of kids have been pacified by the same soppy fable of peaceful repose that Sheridan hooked me with. All my years in the laboratory had taught me better, but I wanted to believe his fairy tale. All of us prefer the prettied-up version of life. And death.

The kids protested, but I shooed them off to a

neighbor's house for the rest of the afternoon and then ducked into my bedroom to change my clothes. My thoughts zoomed ahead. More than anything, I wanted to keep a lid on Aaron's grizzly killing. Just for a little while. Now that he was dead, there was no reason to keep it secret forever. But the coincidence of his slaughter could provide convenient cover for the bear thefts of Kirby Rogers. With better than a dozen grizzlies dead, what's a few more? Even if you can't find the carcasses. Too smooth. No, before the truth came out, Kirby Rogers had to be brought down. To be safe, I decided to leave the bears out of my story completely.

Before we left, Detective Sheridan asked to use the bathroom. I paced the hall, barely noticing that he walked past the kid's bath and used the one off the master bedroom. Probably had kids of his own. That explained it. He knew better. Now if only Aaron Whittier had kept his killing spree to himself. He hadn't mentioned it to the TNC pilot. Who else could he have told?

Those thoughts distracted me all the way into town. The clinical details of the morgue didn't disturb me. Labs are also places of sharp odors and stainless steel, dissection and microscopic slides. The main difference was the colder air. We followed the attendant through a set of double doors and into a room hung with rows of drawers. Just like on TV.

"Whittier, right?" The young man in the white coat snapped his gum. "Came in this morning?"

Sheridan nodded and moved me forward as the attendant pulled open the bottom drawer of the closest row. Undraped, Aaron Whittier's head emerged from the drawer—skin gray and mouth half open, eyes slit and glassy. So much for peaceful repose.

I wobbled, but the detective had an arm around me, and I stayed up. A vision of Roland's bloody bits flashed through my mind. In the end there was little difference between that sight and this one. The horror isn't in the blood and gore. The horror is in the utter stillness and absence of life.

"Yes." The word came out a squawk. "That's him."

Sheridan swung me away before the attendant could get the drawer closed. "Will you come down to headquarters now and make a statement?"

On the way neither of us spoke. I rolled down the window on my side and gulped the fresh air, hoping the rushing stream would wash the clinical stink from my clothes and hair. Killing bears was better than killing yourself. The thought left me feeling like a traitor to my cause.

At police headquarters Sheridan led me into a small office and brought me the worst cup of coffee I've ever attempted to drink. I managed to get most of it down while we talked. The warmth burned away the last of the morgue's icy clutch as I repeated my story, this time for a tape recorder.

Finally Sheridan stopped asking questions and stopped the machine. "So that's your statement?"

I nodded. "Yes."

He glanced away. "And when I give you a transcript, you'll swear to the truth of it and add your signature to the bottom?"

"Sure." I tried a smile. "If you guys get it right."

"What if we have more questions?" His eyes snapped back to my face. "You'll answer?"

"Yes, of course." No reassurance in those blue eyes now. How long had it been gone? What was he getting at? "Do you have more questions?"

"Yeah." He frowned. "Try this one—what happened to your face? Those cuts are pretty fresh. Maybe two days old."

I touched my cheek. "My face? I cut it when I slipped and fell down at McNeil. The grass was covered with dew and I slipped. And fell."

"Yeah?" His eyes told me he didn't believe me.

"Yeah!" I sat forward. "It was dawn and the grass was wet with dew. I came running out when I saw Aaron and slipped. And down I went."

He threw me a sly smile. "You're out in the middle of nowhere. You see a strange man. And you come running out?"

Put that way, the truth sounded phony as hell. Almost the truth. I hadn't mentioned the bear. Now I had no choice. "There was a bear coming. I wanted to warn him."

"Oh, there was a bear coming?" No pretense of believing me now. He wasn't humoring me. He was mocking me. "And then what happened?"

I sat back in the chair and folded my arms. "I don't know, Detective Sheridan. Why don't you tell me?"

He looked at me steady for a couple of seconds and then nodded. "I think you two got tangled up down there. Kind of a kick—strange man, no one around. And it got rough. Too rough, in the end, but you played along. He scared you."

I shook my head but couldn't manage words. I couldn't even breathe. The idea sickened me.

"Flew back together and it was over. Except you

couldn't get over the rough treatment. And then he called. You went to his motel. And you killed him."

Now I *was* scared. One set of facts can yield a thousand scenarios. Even murderous scenarios. Except that Aaron Whittier took sleeping pills! Detective Sheridan had said so.

I reminded him and he just nodded, scaring me further. "Yeah, he overdosed on Seconals—50 milligrams. I found one on the floor. Which was good because I didn't find the bottle in his room. I didn't find it anywhere. Until I got to your house."

His trip to the bathroom. My bathroom! He'd gone through my drawers and found the pills prescribed when Max died. He'd found another "fact." And then he'd concocted an outrageous scenario to fit his collection of stray "facts." Anger and fear combined to inject a hysterical edge into my voice. "This is ridiculous. I've already told you. Aaron Whittier was despondent over his daughter's death. He killed himself. I didn't."

"You're telling me a guy whose daughter was killed by grizzlies turns into such a bear lover he spends his vacation at a game refuge?" He shook his head. "No way. I like my version better. You two tangled."

I'd tangled, all right, but what really got snarled up was the truth, not my face. Detective Sheridan had used my tale to construct a parallel reality that better fit his facts. Keeping secrets would no longer help me get Kirby Rogers. Suddenly I was the one at stake.

22

Matt Sheridan turned out to be a good cop. He listened. Carefully. When he didn't understand, he said so. He gave me all the time I needed to give him the whole truth. And I did. Almost. All I left out was the grizzly grabbing of Kirby Rogers.

"Let me recapitulate here. You tell me if I've got it right." He flipped through his notebook. "You're down at McNeil River to shoot some videotape for the conservation outfit you work for. Promotional material. Save the bears, save the earth, et cetera."

"That's right." I nodded vigorously, improving my salesmanship. This story had to sell. "Grizzlies are the kind of predators that get donors pumped up to send money and letters. We're thinking of offering wildlife videos for paid memberships. The kind of thing *Sports Illustrated* does."

Sheridan rolled his eyes and shook his head. "Okay, it's dawn and you're ready to film. Down the trail comes a grizzly. Before you can start your camera rolling, this strange man appears. He doesn't see the bear, but the bear sees him. So you holler a warning."

More nodding. "Right. But he couldn't hear me over the falls."

Sheridan assumed a patient expression but wasn't a good enough actor to sell the put-on. I shrugged an apology. "Sorry. I'll shut up."

"Thank you." He scanned his notes again. "So you run out and end up falling halfway down the hill, startling both the stranger and the bear. The bear charges and the man opens fire, taking the grizzly down. Then he comes over to you and doctors your face."

He invited confirmation with a raised eyebrow, and I nodded again. "He had a good basic first-aid kit in his backpack."

Now Sheridan nodded. "That checks out. We've got his stuff here."

A wave of relief swept through me. He believed me! I just might pull this off. And if I did, Kirby Rogers was mine.

The detective leaned back in his chair and stretched his arms high over his red head. "The daughter also checks out. I made a few calls while you used the facility. A Jennifer Whittier was killed in a grizzly attack at Katmai National Park last year."

I'd never doubted it. No one who'd seen her father's anguish could have any doubts about the circumstances of her death. Still, I nodded. My story was selling but not yet sold.

Sheridan lowered his arms to the table again. "ADF and G confirms the presence of a dead grizzly at the falls. And they want to hear more about this guy's rampage. They're sending somebody over to talk to you. That okay?"

This time my nod wasn't so eager. I'd been hoping that part of this snarl could slide for a while, long enough for me to nail Kirby Rogers. Once the story of the bear thefts broke, no one at ADF and G would remember to ask why I hadn't immediately notified the authorities of Aaron Whittier's slaughter. Maybe I could plead temporary insanity due to head wounds.

He flipped his notebook closed. "I'd say we're about ninety percent there. This time your story fits the facts a little better. Only a few loose ends. Like for instance, why a gung-ho conservationist like you was ready to let a grizzly killer walk?"

And there it was—the final *Jeopardy* question. No way Sheridan would buy temporary insanity. For once, I decided on simple honesty. "Maybe you had to see him to understand." No theatrics behind my deep sigh this time. "The man was destroyed. Aaron Whittier still walked and talked, but he was dead inside. I lost my husband a couple of years ago, so I know."

If that was news to Sheridan, he hid it rather well. And like I said, he listened well. His silence invited me to continue. "In that situation, people need a reason to go on living, not a legal hassle. No purpose would have been served by punishing Aaron Whittier. He'd already been through hell."

The door behind me opened when I was in mid-spiel and in marched Kirby Rogers, followed more timidly by Julianne Blanchard. I managed to hide the bolt of terror that electrified my nervous system and switched on all the interior warning lights at the mere sight of my own personal demon.

His handsome mouth took on a wicked twist.

"Maybe so, Lauren. But you had no business deciding that on your own. And no authority, either. Decisions like that belong to the duly appointed representatives of the citizens of this state. All you represent is a bunch of wimpy Eastern—"

"That's enough." Matt Sheridan rose slowly to his full height, which left him looking down at Kirby Rogers. "If you came for information, we'll provide whatever we can. But if you're here to parcel out blame, then get lost. I've got no time for whiners today."

Rogers stiffened. Behind him, Julianne Blanchard's mouth opened into a perfect O. Mine probably did, too. I wouldn't know. I couldn't spare a thought for such inconsequentials. Not with a face-off between two alpha males just an arm's length away. I'm not one of those women who like to see men in a physical fight, but I am a scientist, and behavior is part of my brief. Especially aggressive behavior. Both of them looked ready for action—stance wide, arms hanging loose, breathing deep, and eyes wary. Sizing each other up. In the natural world most potential conflicts are defused when one of the combatants signals his peaceful intentions. Grizzlies are likely to expose their necks. Tool-building humans prefer to show that their hands are empty of weapons. Which is what Kirby Rogers did next.

He spread his hands. "Hey, I'm sorry. I'm a little upset." And smiled. "I've got a bear sanctuary to run, and you're telling me I have fourteen dead grizzlies. I'm a little upset, so I got carried away. I apologize."

Nice, huh? Detective Sheridan shook the man's hand and offered him a seat. Was I the only one who noticed the ice in Kirby's smile?

I risked a glance at Julianne Blanchard. Her searching eyes darted over my face. That's when Matt Sheridan finally noticed her and ushered her to the fourth seat at the table. Kirby Rogers ignored them both and addressed his questions to me. "So what is this about, Lauren?"

I wanted to meet his eyes but couldn't. The fear was back. After all, the man had tried to end my life. I'd managed to outrun his bullets the first time, but he'd be aiming for a second chance. I looked, instead, at Matt Sheridan, wishing I could tell him the truth about this man. "I'm not sure what's been said so far."

Sheridan shrugged. "That we've got a suicide who claims fourteen grizzly kills at the sanctuary. And an eyewitness to one."

Kirby Rogers leaned toward me. "You're the eyewitness? What happened? You watched him shoot one and then struck up a conversation about the other bears he'd killed?"

I had to grab the seat of my chair to keep from leaning away from him. "Something like that." I shot a glance at the cop. "You told him about the daughter?"

Sheridan steepled his hands under his chin. "Turns out the guy's daughter was killed by a bear last year down at Katmai National Park. He wanted revenge."

Kirby Rogers gave me an evil grin. "So you had something in common."

The detective started to ask a question, but Rogers got his in first. "Where are the others? So far our guys have turned up only one other carcass. From what's left, that death looks like natural causes."

For some reason, that's when I became conscious of

the weight of Julianne Blanchard's eyes upon me. Maybe she made a little noise or movement that caught my attention. However it happened, I was suddenly aware of her and the importance of making a good showing. I needed her help to bring this man down. Chances were she wouldn't risk her pension on a woman who rolled over easily. That realization restored my nerve.

"Look, Rogers, don't put me on trial. I had nothing to do with this." I waved a finger at him. "I didn't ask where the other bears were killed. I expect he hunted most of them outside the sanctuary boundary. I only know for a fact about three dead bears—the one at the falls and two more up a remote drainage farther north and east. Sound familiar?"

Again the detective started to ask a question only to have Rogers beat him to it. What an actor! My barb didn't even ruffle his smooth exterior. "I'll need a better fix on the location than that."

"Fine. Get me a map and I'll show you the exact spot." It was my turn to smile. So smooth, he almost had me fooled as well. But I knew better. I knew he'd visited the spot at least once and stayed long enough to trash the cabin. "Of course, you could have found the carcasses yourself. If you'd taken the trouble to locate Roland Taft's cabin."

His eyes spit fire. "That was weeks ago. And you never reported it?"

I held my ground, ready to really stick him. "There was nothing to report, Kirby. Two dead bears—so what? Bears die all the time. That's not unusual." I sharpened my shiv. "Even hunting inside a game sanctuary is not unusual. As you should know." His frown was the signal to finish him off. "Catching the hunter is what's unusual. Or used to be."

That's when Matt Sheridan broke things up. He shooed me through the door on the pretext of looking at mug shots. Who needed a photo ID when I'd fingered the body? Turned out he had something else in mind.

He yanked me down the hall, his voice a hiss. "So there's some history here. History you never told me about."

I shook my arm free. "What should I have told you? 'Oh, by the way, Detective Sheridan, there's a guy at ADF and G I simply can't stand?' I didn't invite Kirby Rogers over here. That was your idea."

That didn't lighten his glare one bit. "You're very good, Lauren Maxwell. But I'm better. You're keeping something back. Something big."

Talk about understatement. He'd probably charge me as some kind of accessory when he found out we'd shared a table with a murderer and I'd never said a word. Still, I kept silent. I wanted Kirby my way, which left me nothing to say.

Sheridan rocked back on his heels and folded his arms. "Before I said we were ninety percent of the way there. I want to revise my estimate." He rocked forward into a crouch, bringing his eyes to the level of mine. "Now I'd say we're back to maybe fifty percent. And falling."

The door to the room we'd shared opened again and out walked Kirby Rogers with Julianne Blanchard still dogging his heels. I ignored her and looked from one man to the other. Twin threats, I thought, but only one of them lethal.

I thought wrong.

23

Kirby Rogers moved fast. As soon as I'd pinpointed the approximate location of Roland Taft's cabin on the map supplied by Sheridan, he was off. Julianne Blanchard tried to dawdle long enough for a quick exchange, but his bark of command sent her scurrying after him before we'd had time to trade more than hellos. That performance had me worried all the way home. If she chickened out, I was in big trouble. I had absolutely no evidence that proved Kirby Rogers was the monster I knew him to be. And my damned taunting had probably redoubled his determination to eliminate a major problem—me.

The telephone's jangle carried through the varnished wood of my front door as I fumbled for my house keys. A pattern emerged—three rings followed by a few seconds silence and then three more rings. Funny the caller didn't wait for the answering machine, which picked up on the fourth.

I opened the door, tripped over the backpack I'd left in the hall, and reached the receiver on the second ring of the next series. "Hello?"

"Lauren! Thank God I finally reached you. We've got to hurry. He's already left for the airport!"

The urgency of Julianne Blanchard's words swept me into a whirlwind of action. From that moment on I literally had no time to think. "He's going to McNeil right now?"

"Yes. This time I listened in on part of the call." Her voice rang with a new authority. Taking decisive action does that to people. Hooray! The mouse was gone. "He said that this was absolutely the last time, and it had to be today. If we leave right now, we still have a chance!"

Panic stabbed me and I wailed. "I need transportation!"

Triumph chimed through her answer. "I've got that lined up."

A miracle! That's what it was. The mouse had definitely learned how to roar. She rattled off the directions to a small airstrip south of the city and promised to meet me there.

"You're coming?"

No doubts wavered beneath that firm voice. "Yes, of course. There can't be any foul-ups. This is my last chance."

She had no doubts and neither did I. Who had time for questions? Action was the order of the day. I scribbled a note to Nina and the kids, darted through my room to grab my hiking boots, and scooped up the backpack as I shot through the hall. My Sierra cup slipped loose and fell onto the steps as I locked the front door. I plucked it from the decking and clipped it to my belt. Then into the 4-Runner, and the chase was on.

Life's full of situations that contradict the homilies we learned in childhood. The race is to the swift, lasting peace is a contradiction in terms, and the meek aren't even mentioned in the will. Still, fables haven't been handed down from generation to generation because the stories are flat-out phony. Take the one about the tortoise and the hare, for instance. That dumb bunny grossly underestimated the abilities of his opponent. That happens a lot. Which I was just about to find out.

I didn't even try to hold the Toyota under the speed limit. The race was on. A sea breeze rolled through my opened window and blew my judgment away. Even when the airstrip near Rabbit Creek turned out to be little more than a mown pasture, I didn't question. Even when the transportation turned out to be a helicopter that looked too rickety to fly, I didn't question. Who had time?

When I arrived at the field, Julianne Blanchard pushed open the battered door of a rusty Quonset hangar and signaled me to drive the 4-Runner inside. Then she yanked open the back door of my truck, grabbed my backpack from the seat, and dashed for the chopper. I locked up and scrambled after her. She waved me to the passenger seat, and in I climbed. Then she slid behind the controls and fired up the engine.

A question finally occurred to me. "Who's flying this thing?"

She took hold of the stick. "I am."

She was? The helicopter shuddered once and lifted off. She was.

Uh-oh! That was my first thought. So articulate. *Uh-oh.* The ground fell away beneath us as the chopper gained altitude and speed, heading south by southwest. Remember the hare and the tortoise? Imagine Lauren Maxwell as the dumb bunny and a turtle with the mousy features of Julianne Blanchard. For weeks I'd been chasing Kirby Rogers. Now I discovered that he hadn't even been in the race. The instant analysis that followed my realization had the dread conviction of the doomed. I was history.

Too late! That was my second thought. Which I immediately revised. Not too late. How could it be? I wasn't dead yet. When you're dead, it's too late. I dredged up an aphorism that seemed appropriate. Where there's life, there's hope. That provided a little comfort. Emphasis on little.

The helicopter leveled off a few hundred feet above ground. Too high for jumping. Fortunately, the racket of the engines made conversation virtually impossible. I hadn't decided which approach to take. Maintaining the pretense of Kirby's guilt would certainly buy me some time, but so what? Although I was certain that Julianne had something very unpleasant in mind for me, I was almost as sure that her plan wouldn't go into action until we reached the game sanctuary. It couldn't look like murder, after all. On the other hand, preempting her revelation would give me a temporary advantage. Timewise, at least. Our final battle would begin on my schedule. Maybe she'd even make a mistake.

Our flight path left land behind, instead sailing high

over the glistening mud flats of Turnagain Arm. Near the shore a clam digger stopped his search and waved as we passed overhead. I didn't have the heart to wave back. Julianne Blanchard didn't make mistakes. Her manipulation of me had been nothing short of masterful. The sudden enthusiasm for the chase should have tipped me off. And there were other clues I'd overlooked in my single-minded pursuit of Kirby Rogers. Suddenly I knew with a dreadful certainty that she was the dangerous woman pilot who my son and Travis MacDonald had been searching for all month. No wonder they'd never found her plane or her helicopter in that ramshackle hangar. Just like they'd never find my 4-Runner.

I stared down at the bleak waves below and shuddered. What a fool I'd been. And so blindly sexist! When Aaron Whittier told me a woman was involved in the bear thefts, my assumption that she was a squeeze of Kirby's simply added another justification for loathing him. Julianne Blanchard picked up on my rabid hatred of her boss and mirrored it back, providing yet another clue for me to overlook. Only a very sick woman could work so closely with a man she totally despised. That close proximity gave her easy access to the official documents she'd used to snare me into a secret alliance. Amend that to read *copies* of official documents and no doubt cleverly doctored before being diabolically interpreted for her gullible ally. A scientist, indeed. In this endeavor I resembled the fanatics—bizarros like Chevalier de Lamarck or Trofim Lysenko whose science consisted of crackpot theories backed up by personal opinion. I wanted Kirby Rogers to be guilty, and so he was.

The helicopter skimmed above land again, skirting

the shore of Cook Inlet to travel the length of the Kenai Peninsula. The sunlight streamed golden, a sure sign that the afternoon had waned to the brink of evening. Time. Maybe I had more left than I'd thought. A big chunk of time would be spent just getting to the McNeil sanctuary. And Alaska's short darkness might overtake her before she'd done her dirty work. Julianne would need time for that. She had to take care of me and make it look like anything except murder. An accident, maybe. Or another example of statistical inevitability in human-bear encounters.

On and on we flew, high above whitecaps breaking on the sea and spruce steepling the rocky shore. South, always south, following a Sterling Highway in the sky. At the chopper's controls Julianne alternated between studying the terrain below and matching it to the chart spread across her lap. Only one gauge on the control panel attracted her interest—fuel. My God! Maybe she needed to refuel in Homer! I couldn't stand the suspense, so I leaned toward her and shouted the question above the thrumming of the engine.

She shook her head, not sparing me a glance. "We'll make it without even tapping the reserve."

Despair welled up inside me like a bleak sludge, threatening to clog my throat. Too late. Why bother pretending otherwise? And yet I couldn't stand to blubber like an idiot. I'd stood my ground against a grizzly. I could stand my ground against her.

She jumped when I tapped her elbow. Good. My question gave her a start as well. "I suppose the bogus grant proposal from Roland Taft was something you dreamed up?"

Her eyes darted wildly, scanning my face and the chart in her lap and the airspace before the helicopter. The implication certainly upset her equilibrium. She tightened her grip on the stick with the hand closest to me and sent the other into a deep cargo pocket to draw out a small handgun. She rested it atop the chart, barrel pointing at me.

I forced a yelp of laughter, hoping another surprise would keep her off balance. "You call that a weapon? Looks more like a cap gun."

"I agree that yours makes a bigger impression." Her thin lips curled into a smile. "That's why I left it behind."

Damn. I'd forgotten about the .45 in my backpack. Too late. But I couldn't back down now. Even futile verbal jousting was better than simply waiting. "Hey, Julianne, what about the phony statistics in Kirby's research paper? What happens when the buzz gets loud enough for him to hear? He'll figure it out, you know. Then you'll have to kill him, too."

Zing. That got to her. The knuckles whitened on the hand gripping the stick. My throat ached from shouting, but I couldn't stop now. "You can try, but I wouldn't count on it, Julie dear. You're no match for the great white hunter."

That turned out to be her limit. She swung toward me with a snarl. "That's what they all think. But they're wrong. And soon everyone will know."

In her anger she wobbled the stick and the helicopter slid sideways. I grabbed my seat for balance. "So that's what it's all about—Kirby Rogers?"

Once she started to talk, she couldn't seem to stop. Her rambling monologue continued until we reached the game sanctuary. Her sin was an ancient one—

envy. Kirby Rogers got the job she coveted, the job she deserved. And that wasn't all. Her outrage rang clear above the roar of the engine.

"He never noticed me. Or anything about me. He didn't see that I was good. That I was a woman. He looked right through me."

Add a dash of lust and wounded pride to the original sin of envy. A very handsome man and a very plain woman. Julianne had probably heard all the usual stories about Kirby Rogers, making his failure to hit on her into something very pointed and very personal. And topping it all off was Mama.

"She wouldn't let up. Why didn't I do something? Why didn't I sue? The job should have been mine. She's always been like that. Bossy. Unreasonable. Who'd support her if I went to court and lost my job? For years I've taken care of her, and the only thing that made it bearable was knowing that one day I'd be rewarded for all of my hard work. But when the day came, Kirby Rogers got the job."

Talk about depressing. Who wouldn't be discouraged with a history like that? So Julianne decided to fix Kirby Rogers and her mother at the same time. Decimating the grizzly population at McNeil while he had stewardship would seriously undermine his career. And provide the bucks she needed to escape to a new life far away from her overbearing mother. Then along came Roland Taft with his damned questions.

"He knew it was me. He wasn't good at pretending. After he sent that letter, I went down to see him, but it was too late. Maybe he saw us take a bear. I don't think he knew what to do. But I did."

She approached McNeil from the north, angling off into a huge circling arc over the tundra before the helicopter came in sight of the sanctuary. I recognized the terrain below as the area I'd crossed with Aaron Whittier. We swooped lower, hovering just above the trees as she traced a slow rectangle around her chosen spot. Nothing moved. The usual action at McNeil lay far from this isolated glade.

Somewhere below a hidden culvert trap waited for a final bear. I leaned back against the seat and closed my eyes, bracing for the touchdown on the rocky ground. A sudden sting on my left thigh quickly opened them. Julianne's little gun glittered in her hand. The needle of a small syringe had penetrated the cloth of my pants.

"Sucostrin." Her voice was a hollow echo in my ears. And my bones were melting. "Shuts down the central nervous system."

My arms flapped uselessly when I tried to grab her. And my lips thickened into helplessness. I couldn't even scream.

24

When I came to, I no longer wanted to scream. Which is pretty surprising when you consider the fact that what roused me from my Sucostrin stupor was the fury of the very pissed-off grizzly that now inhabited Julianne Blanchard's culvert trap. Basically, the bear had just two moves—gnawing fitfully on the ripe hunk of bacon that had lured him in or throwing himself against the sides of the trap in a ringing, if futile, attempt to break free. The poor guy looked even more dazed than I. That fact might have offered some comfort had our captor left me free to move. But, as I'd already learned, she didn't make mistakes. I was trussed tightly and staked out for slaughter. She'd bound my feet, propped me upright against a sapling that had straggled into the clearing, and laced my hands together around the slender trunk. Simple, effective, and inescapable. Even a punch-drunk bear would have an easy time making this kill.

I didn't scream and I didn't cry because panic never

works. Score one for me. Maybe the lingering effects of the sedative kept me calm. Or maybe my mind had continued to work when I was unconscious. For whatever reason, I awoke determined to survive. And with the presence of mind to feign sleep until I'd assessed the situation.

I left my chin slumped against my chest and peered through the twilight gloom. The knob on the trap's timer was cocked to the right and counting. But counting what? Minutes? Hours? Damn. Why hadn't I studied the trap more closely when I had the chance? I let the question and my frustration subside without an answer. Timer on. Conclusion: The bear presented no immediate threat. That gave me some time.

Scoping out Julianne Blanchard wasn't so easy. I couldn't locate her! She wasn't in my forward range of vision and a thick screen of hair blinded me on both sides. Damn. Why didn't I wear bangs? I'd have to turn my head, but which way?

The bear's racket drowned any sound she might be making. No help there. Turn which way?

Even when the grizzly stopped bellowing long enough to rip into the bacon, nothing emerged from the brief silence to clue me into her location. Turn which way?

I forced a memory of this clearing into my mind's eye. Trap hidden in scrub, open space embraced by thickets of poplar, a lone sapling off to the right. Turn left! Turn left! She had to be on my left because there wasn't room for the chopper on my right. Turn left.

Turning my head took forever. Centimeter by centimeter, I swung my head left. Slowly, slowly, to make the movement resemble an off-balance slide. Inch by inch, my field of vision widened. Grassy open space.

More grass. Something in the grass. A log? The chopper's skid? Yes! The chopper's skid. Body of the chopper. Window. And door. Open! And Julianne! One leg dangling from the open door. One rifle dangling from her hand.

The sight of that rifle struck me a chilling blow. Most of us respond to disaster with the same trite thought: *"I can't believe this is happening."* For all my bravado, I had, too. And then I saw Julianne Blanchard's rifle. The deadly reality of that weapon hit like a jab to the solar plexus. With awful clarity Julianne's plan became apparent. The timer would open the cage. The grizzly would charge out. Julianne would wound the bear. And the maddened grizzly would make quick work of the nearest human. Me.

That's when I came close to crying, but in the next instant the stars showed me the way. To be more precise, a star. Our star. Our sun. Which rose behind me now with all the pink and purple glory of an Alaska dawn.

The first warming rays touched my shoulders. And off to my left, Julianne Blanchard sighed, checked her watch, and then tipped back her head to catch the light on her face, eyes closed against the brilliant dawn.

Dawn! A blessed dawn that filled my heart with hope even as it filled the day with light. The grizzly grew quiet. Probably finished off the bacon and settled in for a snooze. I couldn't risk moving to find out. Instead, I tested the rope binding my hands and found enough slack to allow me to grasp the handle of my Sierra cup. With luck, that cup would be the next thing filled with light. With time that cup of flashing light could be my salvation. Maybe Julianne

Blanchard had finally made a mistake. With the sun as my source of light and the Sierra cup as my source of reflection, I had a chance. All I needed now was luck and time.

Some would term mine a very slender hope. But consider the whitewater rafter who found himself with a compound fracture of the leg at the bottom of the Grand Canyon. The flash of light from his mirror one mile below the surface of the great basin caught the eye of the pilot of a transcontinental airliner flying thirty-five thousand feet above. And then there's the four air crash survivors treading water in the south Atlantic who managed to alert a passing plane by reflecting the sun off of a credit card. Such stories are legion. And true. Their truth was my lifeline. With a little luck, enough time, and some of the busiest airspace on earth, I figured I just might make it out of there alive.

The Sierra cup hung from my belt above my right hip, easily in reach of my right hand. But I needed my left to steady the cup long enough to catch the light. The trunk of the poplar ground into my spine as I craned my left arm to the limit of its reach. Just far enough for my thumb and index finger to close on the rolled tin lip. Score another for me!

A triumphant shot of adrenaline sent a jitter through my arms and I lost the cup. The rising sun lit Julianne's tipped face, eyes still closed. Deep cleansing breath. And another. Try again for the cup. Right hand on wire handle. Left reaching . . . reaching . . . touching . . . got it! Got it! Don't get cocky. Got it.

For the barest second I let my eyes close as well. And then opened them again to check the motionless Julianne. Could she be sleeping? It had been hours since we left Anchorage. And she probably hadn't gotten much sleep since failing to finish me off the first time she'd lured me to the game sanctuary. Sleeping? The possibility remained just that. Possible. Unproven. A hypothesis I couldn't risk testing. I'd have to move carefully to avoid alerting her.

Careful movement proved to be a necessity due to the awkwardness of my position. I just hoped the little I moved was enough to put the cup at the right angle to catch the sun. That's where luck had to come in. Estimating the sun's angle from the shadow I cast was tough enough. Trying to tip the cup into a matching angle was nothing but guesswork. And I had no way to judge my success. Not only were my eyes and the cup positioned in absolute opposition, but whatever reflection I succeeded in making would also flash away from my line of sight.

The day brightened as the sun rose higher. Degree by slow degree, I sharpened the angle on the Sierra cup. Pure guesswork. Was it enough? No sound from the bear. Or the sky. A bird twittered in the scrub behind the culvert. And still Julianne didn't move.

My fingers ached. The poplar trunk bit into my spine and pinched the flesh of my arm. The bird chirped once and then flew off. I soon longed for sound. Any sound. The crash of waves on the far-off shore. The murmur of a breeze swaying through the spruce. The low growl of the distant river running free.

So powerful was my need that suddenly I heard the river song. Too far away and yet there it was— growling, droning, whining. Whining?

Julianne heard it, too. Her eyes opened. I stiffened. Her gaze narrowed into a squint aimed at the climbing sun, giving me time to forceably relax my posture. Which took some doing once I recognized the whine for what it was. A plane! I risked a twitch of the Sierra cup. And another. A plane!

Julianne swung her other leg out of the chopper's cockpit and hopped to the ground, eyes still raised toward my salvation. Then her gaze dropped, darting in a frantic arc that began with the caged bear and finished with me. I steeled myself against those panicked eyes, managing to hold my slumped posture.

She rammed a cartridge into the chamber and raised the rifle to her shoulder. A scream threatened when she sighted down the barrel. But she swung the rifle away, aiming now toward the caged bear.

I raised my head. No need to pretend. My hands twitched the Sierra cup. No need to hide. Help, help, help. She would wound the bear and the maddened grizzly would make short work of me. Once it got out of the cage.

That thought dampened my burgeoning panic. She'd need two shots to finish it—one to open the cage, one to wound the bear. Suddenly I had all the time I needed. And Julianne's had run out.

"Don't shoot! Julianne, don't shoot!"

She ignored me, sighting down the rifle barrel. The sound of the plane's engine built in the east. Closing.

"Julianne, listen. The bear will come after you. You can't get away. He'll come after the rifle."

Still, she ignored me. She was beyond the reach of reason. And, in the end, I was wrong. One shot was all it took.

As her finger began to tighten on the trigger, the plane roared in overhead, just above the treetops. The rifle barked once. And then Julianne Blanchard screamed. Because the shot tore off the lock and wounded the grizzly. The bear came out of the cage at a dead run.

She yanked the lever, trying to chamber another round. Two yards out, the grizzly launched, leading with his paws. His claws punctured her chest, sending up a spray of blood. His teeth tore at her throat and the spray became a fountain.

And then the plane returned, buzzing the clearing. The grizzly raised his blood-soaked muzzle, still straddling Julianne Blanchard's body. My stomach churned, but I didn't move. Didn't dare even to turn my head.

The plane came around in a tight circle. The grizzly opened his mouth and raised it toward the plane in a snapping challenge. Then he lowered his head, sank his bloody teeth into Julianne Blanchard's shredded flesh, and dragged her body into the scrub behind the chopper.

25

This time I didn't spurn the comfort of Cal Williamson's arms. And he didn't seem to mind my tears or my trembles. He put that plane on the ground fast and bounded out with a look of grim determination. His discovery of my bindings prompted a snort of surprise, but he dug out a pocketknife and sawed through the ropes without any comment. Then he lifted me from the ground and into his arms, cradling me like a baby.

"Poor thing. Poor, poor thing."

That gruff crooning provided oceans of comfort as I shook and sniffed and sobbed and shuddered my way toward composure. He seemed to sense the moment when I'd finally pulled myself together. Without a word he set me on my feet and took a step back.

I swallowed hard to steady my voice. "The bear dragged her away. I can't tell you how horrible—"

The threat of tears interrupted me. He took my

hand and patted it gently. "You been through hell. Try not to think about it." He gave me a little tug in the direction of the plane. "Best we get you home to your people."

I yanked my hand free. "But we can't. We can't just leave her."

Cal Williamson leveled sorrowful blue eyes on me. "I don't know what went on here. I don't know how come that bear got trapped or what that lady was doing with a rifle in a game sanctuary or why she tied you up like that. Don't think I want to know, either."

He paused to clear his throat. "All I know for sure is she's beyond help and you aren't. I got no stomach for tangling with that brownie, so I plan to fly right back out of here. And if you've got the sense the good Lord gave you, you'll come with me."

I couldn't choke down the sob that rose in my throat. Fresh tears spilled down my cheeks. I let Cal Williamson put his arm around me and help me into his plane. While he strapped me in, I stared straight ahead. He taxied the plane back and forth, bouncing across the clearing to flatten the grass, stopping every now and then to clear a rock from our homemade landing strip. Until then I hadn't considered the tremendous risk he'd taken to rescue me—braving an armed woman, a maddened bear, and a small clearing that could have proved too short or too rocky or both. Before trying to take off, he radioed our approximate position to his home base. Then he revved his engines, jammed the stick forward, and went for it. The wheels cleared the tops of the poplars with inches to spare.

He swung the plane in a tight arc around the clearing and then headed east northeast for Homer. I tried to find adequate words to express my gratitude, but in the end only managed to choke out, "Thank you."

He patted my hand again. "Try not to think about it."

That seemed like good advice, so I took it. Nina and the kids guarded the door and the phone while I got in three consecutive mental health days, setting a new personal best in that category. For another two days I concentrated on family things with Jake and Jessie—gardening and biking and swimming—but the intensity of my effort left them both in the dust. Exertion and exhaustion helped keep my mind off the nightmare, but in the end careful examination of the horror is the only healthy way to put it forever to rest.

On the morning of the sixth day, I called ADF&G and made an appointment to see Kirby Rogers. Julianne Blanchard's replacement took the call, sounding rather pert after I'd identified myself. "I know he'll be happy to finally hear from you, Mrs. Maxwell."

Turned out she looked pert, too, from the shiny cap of blond hair and glowing green eyes to the giggle of excitement bubbling through her words and the snapping vitality in each high-heeled step. Kirby probably found her a welcome change from Julianne Blanchard's dour efficiency. I didn't. I wanted Julianne back in that office and off my conscience. I wanted to start everything all over again so I could get things right this time. I wanted the clarity of vision to recognize Kirby Rogers for what he was and Julianne Blanchard for what she'd been. How dare he confound me now by hiring the kind of bouncy bimbo I'd expected a specimen of *Scumbag americanus* to employ! Just exactly what kind of man was he?

"I'm shocked and more than a little hurt, quite frankly." He shook that magnificent head and glanced away. "That you would think me capable of such monstrous behavior."

I'd figured why pretend, but maybe I should have. Detailing the specifics of my suspicions about him probably was mean. But I felt mean, damn it! After all, he'd worked with Julianne Blanchard day in and day out, week in and week out, month in and month out without ever having a clue about who she was or what she felt. Legally and morally, safeguarding the bears and McNeil River and uncovering the crimes of his employees were his responsibility. Kirby Rogers had screwed up, and I ended up paying for it.

Anger cloaks a lot of things. Like sexual attraction. Much later I could admit to having had a heavy case of semi-hots for Kirby Rogers. Which had alarmed me no end. Can you imagine Ralph Nader pairing off with Leona Helmsley? Or Jeanne Kirkpatrick running away with Donald Trump? My gut told me Kirby Rogers and Lauren Maxwell were absurdly mismatched, and those instincts turned out to be right. Kirby Rogers had concrete reasons for every environmental position he took. What he lacked was an appreciation for the spiritual mysteries of the natural world. I wound up with a double dose of exactly that. Which probably means I'll never be a great scientist. On the other hand, that kind of heart is required of all tree-hugging preservationists.

The heart-mind dichotomy was one subject covered when Detective Matthew Sheridan tracked me down at home the next day. He had no direct involvement in the official investigation of the goings-on at McNeil River but wanted to apprise me of his findings concerning the death of Aaron Whittier.

"The Blanchard woman's mother refused me entry until I got a judge's order to search." He tilted back in one of my kitchen chairs, looking quite smug. "Turns out I had the right scenario and the wrong perpetrator. Aaron Whittier OD'd on Seconals. And Julianne Blanchard gave him the dose. Found the empty bottle in her medicine cabinet with his prints on it."

My stomach cramped, but it couldn't have showed because he blundered right along. "Two things I can't figure. How she managed to get his prints on that bottle and how she got to him in the first place?"

I'd already told Matt Sheridan everything. In telling him the truth this time, I'd been careful to specify the omissions in my earlier version of events at McNeil River. He'd already spent a good quarter hour berating me for letting my "soft heart" overrule my "lame brain." I'd even promised to go straight to the police next time I ran across a death that looked like murder. Suddenly that promise sounded like one worth fulfilling.

Why pretend? The worst part wasn't finding out that Julianne Blanchard had killed Aaron Whittier. Or even learning that my mistake had cost not one but two lives. I was still too numb to feel the pain of that knowledge yet. Which meant the worst part was admitting my mistake out loud. It usually is.

"I'm not sure about his fingerprints, but I know how she got to him." Matt Sheridan's eyebrows shot up. I took a deep breath and let it sigh back out.

"Through me. I told her his name when she called that night."

He considered not balling me out. I could see the thought arise in his mind and then find easy dismissal. Who could blame him? I may be a scientist, but I'm no crime stopper. And that's exactly what I told Matt Sheridan in an effort to forestall another lecture.

"Of all people, I should know that no investigation is as simple as those portrayed in mystery novels or television shows." As his eyes warmed with my praise, I warmed to my subject. "And knowing that, I should just let guys like you go ahead and do your jobs. From now on, I will."

And right then, I even meant it.

MALICE
DOMESTIC

Anthologies of Original
Traditional Mystery Stories

1

Presented by the acclaimed Elizabeth Peters.
Featuring Carolyn G. Hart, Charlotte and Aaron Elkins,
Valerie Frankel, Sharyn McCumb, Charlotte Maclead
and many others!

And Coming in May 1993

2

**Presented by bestselling author Mary Higgins
Clark.** Featuring Gary Alexander, Amanda Cross,
Sally Gunning, Margaret Maron, Sharon Shankman
and many more!

**Available from
Pocket Books**

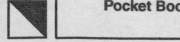